Christelle Angano

Moonlight Serenade over the Channel

elephantsetpattesdemouche.com

Christelle Angano is a French author.

Through her works, she enjoys taking her readers on a journey—not only through her beloved Normandy, but also to more distant lands. She also addresses social issues, on which she does not hesitate to take a stand. She places great importance on the work of remembrance and has dedicated a trilogy, The Clara Cycle, to her great-grandmother. Clara Matthews Chompton, a British-born woman who became a naturalised French citizen, was arrested following a denunciation and died in deportation for helping paratroopers from the British 9th Battalion during D-Day.

In 2022, she chose to leave the national education system to dedicate herself entirely to writing and founded her own business, Éléphants et pattes de mouches.

She now devotes herself fully to writing, leads workshops, and has also decided to expand her work as a ghostwriter.

Traduction par Martin Long de *L'harmonica le trombone et le parapluie* (même auteure), publié aux éditions In Octavo, avril 2024

Couverture et mise en page par Amélie Quermont - Relectrice, Correctrice (www.ameliequermont.com)

© Christelle Angano, 2025
Tous droits réservés
Édition : BoD · Books on Demand,
31 avenue Saint-Rémy, 57600 Forbach, bod@bod.fr
Impression : Libri Plureos GmbH,
Friedensallee 273, 22763 Hamburg (Allemagne)
ISBN : 978-2-3225-6190-2
Dépôt légal : Mai 2025

The little boy
and the paratrooper

Preface

Much is written about the gallant French Resistance during the Second World War, but resistance took on more forms than solely armed opposition, for instance the crucial intelligence gathering prior to D-Day. Another facet that does not receive too much attention are the actions of the many 'ordinary' French people who were not active resistants, but ultimately risked their lives, and those of their families, to help members of the 6th Airborne Division that had been dropped wide during the early hours of D-Day, many landing miles beyond their designated Dropping Zones.

Christelle has produced a beautifully written and poignant tale that reflects, in one such incident, the many legacies of this bravery; one of them being love. She relates in a masterful manner the depth of pain that can go with such love, engendered and exaggerated during wartime. This book is a tribute to all such French people and I commend the author in the writing of it.

Neil Barber

Neil Barber

Neil Barber is a British historian specialising in the airborne operations of the Second World War, particularly those carried out by the British 6th Airborne Division in Normandy. He is the author of several reference works, including The Pegasus and Orne Bridges: Their Capture, Defence and Relief on D-Day and The Day the Devils Dropped In. These works provide detailed accounts of the strategic capture of the Bénouville and Ranville bridges, as well as the actions of British airborne troops on D-Day. With over 30 years of experience, Barber has interviewed many veterans and explored battlefields to enhance his research. He also shares his expertise by guiding tours of the historical sites linked to the 6th Airborne Division in Normandy.

He is a respected member of the 9th Parachute Battalion Reunion Club, and a former member of the Merville Battery Museum Committee.

Report from Sergeant Smith (a genuine document) :

'We took off for Normandy on June 5, 1944, at 11:15 PM.

At 1:00 AM on June 6, I landed in a forest west of Barneville.

[Barneville la Bertran, author's note.] I sprained an ankle upon landing. Of course, I immediately tried to contact my section and recover the containers. Without success. So, I stayed hidden in that forest until dawn, then headed north. I then encountered a Frenchman who was able to inform me of my position. I had to stay in the forest for another eighteen hours before heading south this time.

After two hours, I found Corporal Wilson, himself hidden in a hedge. We stayed hidden there until June 7. At 7:00 PM, we began to move southwest. In the evening, a German sentry fired at us, forcing us to hide in a cornfield until dawn. We were then able to resume our journey, and around 8:00 AM on June 8, we managed to take refuge in the forest of Saint Gatien des Bois, where we stayed until June 9.

As we headed towards Saint-Benoît, we met two women who agreed to help us. They returned with their brother and brought provisions. We stayed hidden in a forest near Saint-Benoît until June 12.

During these three days, the Frenchman brought us sustenance: some blankets and provisions.

Finally, on June 12, a member of the Resistance arrived at our hiding place and took us by truck to a barn about three kilometres east of Honfleur, where we stayed until June 25, before a group of about thirty resistance fighters took us to a house near Manneville. On July 9, we were taken once again, still by truck, to a barn four kilometres north of Beuzeville.

Eventually, the two men managed to return to the United Kingdom at the end of August 1944, after, as we have seen, being cared for by the Resistance and regularly moved to throw off pursuers.

Meanwhile, four or five other paratroopers stayed in Barneville-la-Bertran, taken in by local families.

Clara Matthews Chompton was of English origin; she acted as an interpreter and, like others, helped with supplies. Thus, a part of the community came to the aid of the English, hiding them, feeding them, and providing them with clothing.

Clara was my great-grandmother.

I (albeit very freely) drew inspiration from the story of the paratroopers of the 9th Battalion and Clara's tale to write this novel, which I dedicate to them.

'Music washes away the dust of everyday life.'
— Art Blakey

'Friendship is certainly the finest balm for the pangs of disappointed love.'
— Mark Twain

PART ONE

1994

Moonlight serenade

Chapter 1

Grand-Bourg-Lès-Essart, December 14, 1994
Pension Les Sources

The hoarse ringing of an old alarm clock echoed in the small room. With a swift motion, Peter Gordon silenced it, but the ticking, unperturbed, soon resumed. Now awake, the man put on on his slippers, placed neatly under the bed, and with a hesitant gait, made his way to the bathroom. It was the walk of a man marked by life, memories, and certainly, regrets.

On the old-fashioned sink lay a straight razor, a shaving brush, and soap. Above it, a small, cracked mirror hung from a simple chain. Everything was ready. With a familiar gesture, Peter Gordon ran a hand over his chin to feel the roughness of a burgeoning beard. A perfect shave was a matter of honour for him, and over time, this morning ritual had become a solemn ceremony.

One final step : the music. An old Glenn Miller record, his idol. Now, everything was ready.

The actions followed an immutable order : the

blade sharpened on the worn leather strap, cheeks lathered, and finally, the cold caress of the razor. The motion was slow, sure, instinctive. For the old man, shaving each morning was a way to reconnect with life, to emerge from a night now filled with ghosts ; those of his friends had fallen in the war, and from whom he had never truly been able to part company. Emily's ghost as well. That persistent feeling of being there, almost like a thief, illegitimate in a way, had never left him. Yes, seeing his face reappear as the soap dissolved, like fog lifting, was like reclaiming himself – a grave, solemn, and always somewhat painful moment.

Once dressed and closely shaved, he headed to the kitchen and prepared his breakfast. A large bowl of black coffee, two slices of toast. The butter was soft, almost rancid, the bread nearly hard. But the old man couldn't stand waste. 'Bread and butter shouldn't be wasted, especially when you've known what it's like to go without,' he often said.

*

Peter Gordon

Planes had always been Peter Gordon's passion ; flying, his fantasy. In those great birds he saw friends that allowed him to dream, and the pilots were heroes of modern times. When, as an adolescent, life at the Walsall Orphanage became unbearable, and the thick, cold walls seemed to close in on him until he felt suffocated, he imagined himself at the controls of one of those machines. His hero at the time was Douglas Bader, a passionate pilot who had lost both legs in a stunt accident but had, nonetheless, rejoined the Royal Air Force at the start of the war. His handicap earned him the nickname 'The Legless Ace' back then. The young Peter Gordon was deeply impressed by the aviator's courage and determination. Unfortunately, joining the prestigious No. 1 Flying Training School RAF was very difficult, especially when growing up in a Midlands orphanage, two hundred kilometres from London.

During the war, he joined the 9th British Parachute Battalion, one of those that landed in Normandy. Once peace returned, he settled in London where he found a job as a mechanic at Heathrow Airport. It was his way of continuing to dream. Later, however, he left the world of aviation to enter the world of music, his other passion, and became a salesman in a music shop, 'The Paradise for Musicians,' on the famous Denmark Street. There, he could spend hours talking about clarinets and trombones, his favourite instruments, and he became friends with the owner, an old bachelor who was a jazz enthusiast and who had dedicated his life to music. Those were good years, and Peter finally blossomed. One morning, a young man walked into his shop to buy his first guitar. What pride for Peter to recount, years later, that he had helped George Harrison, the Beatles's guitarist, chooses his first instrument ! When the old owner died a few years later, he bequeathed his shop to Peter. And yet, despite the success of his business, Peter felt it was time to move on. France attracted him. That's where he wanted to live.

He went there every year, in June and December. As a veteran, he wouldn't miss the call for the 'DDAY' commemorations for anything in the world. In Merville-Franceville, at the site of the battery, he made a habit of honouring the memory of his fallen friends.

He discovered the small town of Douvres la Délivrande, on the Côte de Nacre. At that time, he was searching for the grave of a childhood friend with whom he had grown up in the orphanage and who had been lost at the beginning of the war. He eventually learned that his friend had fallen in this small town in Normandy. That's where he rested. Peter made it a habit to come 'visit him' every year – his expression – most often standing silently and respectfully at the grave. Sometimes, often, he would take out his harmonica to play a very solemn 'God Save the Queen.'

He ended up selling his shop to settle on the Côte de Nacre, finding work as a guide in a small museum, and becoming a translator and correspondent for the Ouest-France newspaper. He lived there for many years, in a pretty stone village house, with a small garden where he spent hours dreaming about the past with Winston, his dog, by his side. When he wasn't dreaming in his garden, he was out drawing. He always carried a sketchbook and a pencil, sharpened with a knife – Peter Gordon hated pencil sharpeners. If one could flip through his sketchbook, they would find a recurring smile, like a refrain. Always the same : a slightly sad, mysterious smile, but one that had something that made you want to believe in the future. There, he was appreciated by all. 'The Englishman,' as he was affectionately nicknamed, was a rather solitary and discreet man, about whom little was known, except that he had arrived there one day, almost by chance, and never left. He was often seen at the Baronnie, a former seigneurie of the Bishopric of Bayeux. He loved this place steeped in history, imagining William the conqueror and his friend, Archbishop Thomas of Dover, the first Archbishop of York. The magnificent building had served as a dispensary in 1944, and of course, this could only touch his paratrooper's heart.

One morning, however, while drinking his coffee in the bar on his street, a small ad in Ouest-France changed everything: 'Grand-Bourg-Lès-Essart, opening of the boarding house "Les Sources" in the former boys' school.

He quickly called. Everything happened very fast. When registering, he insisted on occupying Studio 22. Studio 22 and no other. It was the *sine qua non* condition for him to move in. He was even ready to pay the price for his demand. Why 22 ? '22,' he simply replied. *Madame* Martin thought the future resident must be quite an original character and accepted. After all, it seemed important to him. He continued, insisting that the beams not be repainted and that the stone walls remain visible. The owner, a little surprised by these new requests, promised to do so. Relieved, the old man added that he would remember it… when the time came.

Thus, it was without regret that he left the village house where he had settled so many years earlier. He left without looking back. The time had simply come to start a new chapter, the last one, probably. Sometimes, one shouldn't overthink things.

*

On the morning of December 14, it had been exactly one month since he had moved in. *Madame* Martin had welcomed him eagerly. He was 'her first Englishman', she pointed out with a broad smile. He wouldn't regret his choice and would enjoy his new 'Home, sweet home.' The 'Les Sources' boarding house… She placed great importance on this term. Boarding house, not a retirement home, and certainly not a nursing home. Everything there had been thought out, designed, and conceived to make one feel comfortable. The place was pleasant, well organised, offering all the necessary comforts to its thirty residents who could no longer or did not want to live alone ; a true living space, even if, for some, life now moved at a slower pace.

The main half-timbered house was an old building reserved for communal living. It comprised a lounge for residents who wanted to watch television, a music room with an upright piano and a dance floor, a reading room, and finally, a pretty and well decorated dining room, for those who wished to dine together. Three outbuildings converted into studios, one of which was reserved for couples, completed the estate. Each building was connected to the main house by awnings, which protected the residents from bad weather or the sun's heat. At the centre, there was a large shaded courtyard with old oak trees, where a fountain and benches had been installed. In good weather, one could stroll in the orchard adjacent to the house and even rest by a small stream that ran through it. Madame Martin had placed a few picnic tables there. In summer, they were available to everyone. It allowed for socialising when children's laughter mixed with the crystalline song of the water, much to the delight of all.

Peter Gordon quickly adapted to his new life. Curiously, it was as if he were rediscovering a familiar place. He enjoyed walking along the stream, drawing in the chair under the awning, playing the trombone sometimes, the harmonica often. He took his meals in his studio and went out regularly. He had quickly put a certain distance between himself and the other residents, whom he called 'the old folks.' Indeed, approaching 75, Peter did not see himself in these new neighbours, whom he found worn out by this time. No, he had moved into Studio 22 as one moves into a residence, certainly not a retirement home. It was different. At least, for him.

This morning of December 14, lost in his thoughts, he was getting ready. As every year, he was expected in Étretat. The time had come to reunite with Colette and Léo, and also the Hôtel de l'Aiguille. Over the years, he had not missed many of these appointments. Over time, this visit had been taken on the semblance of a pilgrimage.

Chapter 2

Étretat, December 15, 1994

A cold and windy day was dawning over the city. The storm had raged for several days, and, as often in this season, the English Channel had spilled into the streets, covering the promenade with its foam. While tourists were still nestled in the cosy warmth of their hotel rooms, Peter Gordon was already facing the sea, standing straight, his gaze fixed on the horizon. Neither the cold seemed to affect him nor the sea spray bother him. With great care, he descended the few steps separating him from the round, slippery pebbles. The hypnotic backwash rocked the gulls and seagulls, as well as the few boats still asleep on the beach. The waves softened, as if to welcome him. The man raised his hand to his forehead in a very solemn salute to the cliffs before pulling his harmonica from his pocket. The music mingled with the backwash. There was something magical about this communion. Meanwhile, imperceptibly, the sky, bit by bit, prepared to welcome the sun, adorning itself with colours that only Norman skies know how to offer to those who appreciate them. Soon, the chapel of Notre-Dame de la Garde would bathe in the light.

Peter Gordon had a habit of staying at L'Hôtel de l'Aiguille, and had done so for decades. It was his foothold. A simple place where he liked to rest, away from the tumult of a world that overwhelmed him. The hotel was small : five rooms, a dining room, and 'the boudoir' with its pretty stone fireplace. The furniture, though a bit old-fashioned, was nonetheless charming, with its faded tapestries and slightly worn armchairs that welcome you with open arms. One felt at ease here. This was certainly due to the personality of Colette, a young, considerate, and gentle woman, always attentive, discreet, and, on top of that, an excellent cook. She and her younger brother, Léo, had been raised by their grandmother after their parents' death. It was their grandmother who had initiated Colette into the art of cooking. Now, the brother and sister were alone, and Colette had taken over the restaurant. At the time, Léo had begged her not to send him to boarding school. He would stay in Étretat and help her with the hotel ; she needed him. Who would fetch the firewood if he left ? Who would protect her too ? He had said this with such vehemence that she couldn't help but give in. Thus, the young boy now attended middle school a few kilometres away in Fécamp, and the rest of the time, he helped his sister or dreamed on the beach, tossing pebbles into the water. The two were rarely apart, and people loved seeing them walk together through the streets. The boy was as tall as his sister was short, as blond as she was brunette… One common feature, however : a vast blue gaze that devoured their faces and captured your heart.

Peter always reserved the same room, with a view of the sea; and this, for fifty years now. Over time, Colette had grown attached to this special client she had known since she was a little girl. He often came accompanied by his friend Ruby, an old lady with incredible outfits and laughter. However, if they came together, each had their own room. This year, though, he had come alone, which had worried the young woman. She had therefore asked her brother to spend the day with their old friend, especially when he would climb the cliff, which he would undoubtedly do. That too was a ritual.

*

At his sister's request, Léo joined their guest on the beach, passing the time by throwing stones into the water.

— It's chilly. You'll catch a cold. Come on, Mr. Peter, Colette is waiting for us.

The boy grabbed the musician's hand and helped him up the slippery steps. In just a few more meters, they would soon be warm. As always, a hearty breakfast awaited them in the hotel kitchen. A large bowl of hot coffee and a chocolate, a few slices of toast, and a glass of juice – nothing better to prepare for a winter day. Peter Gordon then retired to his room, which he was pleased to find just as he had left it. Everything was in its place. Colette had made sure it wasn't too warm, 19°, no more, no less. Instinctively, he went to the window and opened it wide. He stood there for a moment, inhaling the iodine and gazing at the now-pink sky. Who would have believed that just three days earlier, a storm had battered the coast, with furious waves crashing for hours ? But, as always, Étretat, stoic, had withstood the assault, relying on the next day and, of course, on the Virgin Mary, protector of sailors.

Turning around, Peter noticed the old magazine dedicated to Glenn Miller left for him on the side table the previous day. Smiling, he picked it up, touched by Colette's gesture, and settled into the small armchair. Soon, his gaze drifted off into the distance. He was young, on a street in London, and the future was his. It all seemed so close… and yet, so distant. But the old man shook his head. It was never good to get lost in such memories. After all, he was happy to be here. Colette and Léo were like the family he never had.

If only Emily…

No, he must not think of Emily. He would turn his thoughts to her later. For now, it was time to do what he had come for, once again. Perhaps for the last time. Slowly, he prepared himself. The time had come for him to return to the great cliff of Aval.

The tourists, now awake, filled the cafés and

hotel restaurants where croissants, coffee, and other hot drinks awaited them. The more adventurous had already started their ascent up the paths to the cliffs. Meanwhile, restaurant owners were preparing their tables for lunch. It was the season for crabs and oysters. Platters of seafood, all more appetising than the last, delighted the eye and the palate. Pyramids of shellfish were displayed for hungry eyes. Some preferred velvet crabs, others swore by spider crabs. The impatient chose the easier-to-peel crabs, the gourmets preferred the refined taste of velvet crabs, and in spring, the local speciality was *"moussettes"*, even if it meant going to the Cotentin or Granville to get them. As for oysters, connoisseurs swore only by those from Grandcamp-Maisy.

Chapter 3

The pale sun now pierced through the milky blanket of clouds. The sky, mirrored by the sea, resembled a Monet painting. A light breeze caressed the greenery, making it sway with pleasure. The gentle waves harmonised with the moment. The most courageous souls had braved the cold and the stairs and were now strolling along the cliffs, while the gulls and seagulls shared the wind. Parents held their children's hands, some daredevils amused themselves by getting dangerously close to the edge.

Kids perched on their fathers' shoulders laughed, while infants stayed warm in comfortable baby carriers. People crossed the footbridge to hide in the small shelter, taking photos. Some, the more whimsical, imagined themselves uncovering Arsène Lupin's treasure in the hollow needle.

Waves of tourists, waves of foam, everything was in motion.

The climb proved difficult, perilous even. The wind had picked up, and the ground seemed ready to give way at any moment under the old man's unsteady feet. While the view was fantastic, they had no time to appreciate it. Peter clung to his young companion's arm, breathless, his legs wobbly. He was acutely aware of the years that had passed, weighing him down, slowing him. They were present in his aching knees, his stooped shoulders, and his blue-veined hand gripping Léo's arm. In truth, Peter had never felt so old, and it suddenly became clear that he would not be taking this so familiar path, again.

Once they reached the top, it took him longer than he would have liked to catch his breath. Finally, he pulled his harmonica from his pocket, and soon, the first notes of 'Moonlight Serenade' floated into the air. The wind, perhaps softened by the nostalgia of the tune, became a breeze, and the seagulls joined in a suspended ballet. Even the swell seemed to calm : nature itself held its breath.

— Sir Gordon, why do you always play that piece when you come up to the cliff ? And why always on December 15 ?

The Old man paused

— You noticed, didn't you ? You're right. You know, a great man died off these cliffs. His name was Glenn Miller. He was my friend. If you want,

I'll tell you the story tonight, but not now. Now, I must play. For him.

Léo couldn't help but feel proud. He felt like he was discovering his friend anew, who, until now, he had seen as just a lonely old man. Of course, he had heard of Glenn Miller from his grandparents, and he had to admit, this revelation of their friendship impressed him greatly.

The pieces flowed one after the other, and the wind, a conspiratorial messenger of these musical reunions, carried the notes. They were soon joined by a few walkers : lovers holding hands, more athletic hikers taking a break… Some dared a few dance steps. An older woman discreetly wiped away a tear, transported back to a past she thought she had forgotten. She remembered the young girl she had been, that evening at the dance where she met the man who would become her husband ; the companion the war had ultimately taken from her, whom she had never been able to forget. It was a timeless moment, a welcome parenthesis.

Soon, a few violin notes joined the harmonica's melody. It was Julie Anne. She was well known here. Peter approached the young woman. The walkers applauded, delighted by this impromptu concert.

At the end of the 'performance', Peter Gordon bowed to his charming partner. To thank her, he invited her to join them at the Hôtel de l'Aiguille for dinner. Somewhat surprised but touched, Julie Anne accepted. As they descended, it was Peter's turn to question Léo. Did he know her ? Yes, he knew her. She had moved there a few years earlier, living in a large house at the top of the cliff, alone, with a dog that accompanied her everywhere. A former Parisian, she had left everything on a whim to settle in Normandy. She was a very secretive, somewhat introverted woman. She often said that her cello and violin were her best friends. To make a living, she gave music lessons to children and adults. Today, she had become a true Etretataise. She was a bit like Peter, playing on the beach, on the cliffs, everywhere. Sometimes, she gave concerts in the chapel and in small venues on the Côte Fleurie, mostly classical music. She had befriended Colette and taken a liking to young Léo, her student. She was thus a regular at the hotel restaurant, accompanied by Tantale, her golden retriever. To be honest, Peter was troubled. Her smile reminded him of another smile, those hands of other hands... And that auburn hair... another head of hair... which had haunted him for so many years. But no, Peter, you old fool, those hands, that smile, that fiery hair belonged to a bygone era.

*

The tourists had now fled the seashore to crowd into the shops. Christmas was approaching : it was time for shopping. The main street smelled of roasted chestnuts and mulled wine. The town's loudspeakers played the obligatory Christmas carols on a loop. All of Étretat seemed to have gathered at the Covered Market. There, the stalls were brimming with knitwear. A froth of warm, colourful hats, tendrils of caressing scarves, a foam of cosy, reassuring sweaters, protective gloves – everything here was an invitation to be comfortable At the entrance to the market, a barrel organ competed with traditional songs. Here,

Riton was as well known as the cliffs, just as old too, or so he claimed. With long white hair, a belly held in by suspenders, and a sailor's cap pulled low over his eyes, he was a local celebrity. *Mademoiselle* Paulette, the market's longest-serving vendor, was an ageless spinster whom everyone liked, but whom they still teased a bit. The elders said that *Mademoiselle* Paulette had once been engaged to a fisherman from Fécamp, but the sea, a jealous rival, had decided otherwise. For years, Paulette had stubbornly wandered the cliffs, hoping to see the long-awaited trawler return. But time had passed. Today, *Mademoiselle* Paulette sold hats and sailor sweaters. The lack of love had withered her, and she had become as ugly as she had once been beautiful.

By the sea, the illuminated casino had opened its doors to dreamers and the daring. People entered full of hope, alone or in groups, convincing themselves that 'this time would be the one', that it was the moment to hit the jackpot, a foretaste of Christmas. There were the passing visitors and then the regulars. The latter were easily recognised : grandmothers in their Sunday best, men in sharp suits who wasted no time and went directly to their favourite slot machine. The atmosphere was electric, the white lights and the noise of the slot machines ensnared you, pressed you before casting you back into the cold, tired of believing, but with a firm decision to return and try your luck again the next day.

*

Peter, meanwhile, would spend the afternoon in his room. He needed to rest. The morning on the cliff, the climb, the music, Julie Anne… It was a lot of emotion for his tired heart. He needed to regain some strength for the evening. Tonight, he would have guests. After a short, restorative nap, he sat at the small table and took his old, yellowed sketchbook out of his bag. Always the same face, drawn in pencil. Hair in waves, an enigmatic smile, eyes veiled by lowered eyelids, high cheekbones, a clear forehead. Like all the others, the portrait was unfinished. Perhaps it was an outline of happiness. As always, the pencil strokes were gentle, the artist's smile nostalgic. A small room in a half-timbered house, a piano… Life had passed, yet all it took was picking up his pencil to recapture every emotion, every sensation from that June evening in 1944 – Careful, Peter, don't get too carried away in your memories. It's always hard to come back, and tonight, you have guests ! – He stood up with a sigh, walked to the window, and opened it wide. He needed to breathe, close his eyes, and offer his face to the winter cold to reconnect with the present. From there, he could hear the waves rolling over the pebbles, the murmur of the town, the laughter of children. Life was indeed there, at his feet. And he was alive. Once again, he thought about the evening ahead. He, who had always kept everything buried deep inside, now felt the need to tell, to share, to pass on. Moving into the retirement home a few weeks earlier, meeting the charming violinist, the impromptu concert on the cliff… Yes, the time had come to share. And once again, a sudden realisation : it was the last time he would come to Étretat. Yet he felt no sadness, just perhaps, a hint of nostalgia.

That's how it was, and he had to accept it.

His reverie was interrupted by Colette knocking at his door. He opened it with a somewhat forced smile.

— Here, Mr. Gordon, I've made you some hot tea. A 'Yorkshire' ; I believe it's your favourite. I've also added two slices of my French toast. I know you like it.

— Come in, Colette. You remember well. Do you have a few moments to spare ? Let's share this snack. Nothing would please me more. And besides, I'd like to talk to you.

Noting the somewhat solemn tone, the young woman closed the door behind her and placed the tray on the table.

— Tell me, Colette, tonight, I would like you to dine with us. Do you think you could free yourself ? You're my guest. Perhaps you could ask someone to cover for you in the kitchen… The cellist… Julie Anne, that's right, will also be joining us…

Without really knowing why, Colette sensed some urgency in this invitation and accepted.

— You may not know, but I first stayed at this hotel on December 14,

1947... 47 years, I've been a loyal guest. Since then, I don't think I've missed a single visit. But that, you already know.

Once again, memories resurfaced. Peter recounted the hotel's early days when it was run by the young woman's grandmother, his meeting with her grandfather in the 1950s. Peter had known the whole family, Colette and

Léo's parents, their marriage, the birth of both children, and then the accident when Léo was only two months old, Colette twelve.

His memories were like so many gifts. Colette felt like she was reconnecting with her parents, her mother's sweet perfume, her father's passion for motorcycles, their hearty laughter, and the strong love that united them. Then he spoke of Suzanne, their grandmother. She had been his friend, the most faithful, the most intimate too. Did Colette know ? They had met when Peter first came. That's how Hôtel de l'Aiguille became his home base.

— I have something for you, Colette. Oh, it's not much, but I wanted to give it to you. It belongs to you. And I think it's time for me to pass it on.

He pulled a folder from his bag and took out a drawing. Tears immediately welled up in the young woman's eyes. A woman and a little girl were smiling at her. She immediately recognised the gentle smile of Suzanne ; she gently caressed the smile of the little girl. Yes, it was her mother and grandmother looking at her.

— It looks like Léo when he was little, she

managed to say, her voice choked.

She remained silent for a long time, then composed herself :

— I need to go and prepare everything for tonight. I'll see you later. Thank you again, Mr. Peter. May I give you a hug ?

She placed a childlike kiss on the old man's cheek and left the room, swiftly brushing her tears away.

Chapter 4

The restaurant dining room reflected the hotel's atmosphere : simple and friendly, with about ten tables, no more, covered with traditional red and white chequered tablecloths. It was more than sufficient. No frills, just a convivial, family-like atmosphere. There were regulars, such as old Francis who couldn't bear his recent widowhood, the travelling salesman prospecting in the region, a trucker in transit, and *Mademoiselle* Paulette.

Some even had their napkin rings engraved with their names. This was the case for Julie Anne. People loved coming to Colette's place because they found something there that evoked family. A few customers were already present. It was 7 p.m., and the service would begin soon.

Peter made his entrance, smiling with satisfaction. Elegantly dressed in a tweed jacket, his hair neatly combed, freshly shaved, he smelled of soap and aftershave. His table, always the same one, slightly apart near the hearth, awaited him. Colette led him there.

— I'll be right with you, she whispered.

He was soon joined by Julie Anne and Léo. She moved gracefully through the tables, preceded by her dog. The room fell silent, admiring the young woman, her slender figure perfectly highlighted by a dress whose dark green accentuated the fiery glow of her hair. The atmosphere was serene, the meal cheerful and lively. The four friends enjoyed a fish soup followed by a beautiful sole with steamed potatoes.

— How did you come to know Glenn Miller ?

— Léo, what's got into you ?! That's not very polite !

— Let him be, Colette. No problem. He's right. I promised him… You want to know ? Yes, I'll tell you. It's an old story… Actually, I owe it all to my friend Ruby, whom you know. But let's 'start at the beginning'. That's how you say it, right ? I'll tell you about the first time I came to your country… The first time… But tell me, shall we have our dessert in the lounge ? I overdid it a bit today, I think, and I wouldn't mind sitting in one of your armchairs.

While their friend settled in, Léo lit a fire. Colette, meanwhile, offered some herbal tea that would nicely end the meal.

— Would you have anything stronger ? I wouldn't mind a small whisky. A Glenmorangie would be perfect. We'll drink to friendship.

Peter settled into a comfortable armchair, Julie Anne did the same. At her feet, the golden retriever fell asleep. Colette returned with the bottle of honey-coloured whisky and three glasses. Léo fetched a glass of soda.

Everything was ready. After a long silence, Peter began to speak :

— At the time, I was living in London. I had reconnected with my childhood friend, Ruby. She had joined the Red Cross to care for the wounded during the blitz. You may know that we grew up together in the Walsall Orphanage, in a small town in the West Midlands. When I found her, Ruby Allister had undeniably become a charming Londoner.

— How did you find each other ? asked Léo.

— Fate had us take refuge in the same shelter during an air raid. At the time, Ruby was making a living working as a waitress in a bar. We were in the midst of war, bombings were regular, and the D-Day landings were eagerly awaited. We were exhausted by the carnage. We were young and wanted to live and have fun. And we were scared, too. In late May, I was finally called up. I had to prepare and join the Broadwell base about a hundred kilometres from London. I have always loved planes, I dreamt of flying. So, I enlisted in a parachute battalion.

— You were a paratrooper ?

The boy's eyes widened in amazement. In admiration, too.

— Yes… In the 9th Battalion, to be exact. What do you think ?! I haven't always been an old man ! Well, buckle up, I'm starting my story…

PART TWO

1944
In the mood

Chapter 5

'It has been a big week for us. Over there on the beaches of Normandy, our boys have fired the first shots of the long-awaited campaign to liberate the world.'
— Glenn Miller, June 10, 1944

Military Airfield of Broadwell, June 5, 1944, around 11 PM

It was time. The Dakotas roared along the runway. Our mission was to prepare the Sword sector so that Operation Overlord could succeed. For that, we had to take down the enemy battery at Merville-Franceville. We had been there for several hours, waiting in the rain, encouraging each other, patting each other on the back, whistling to maintain our composure. The load was heavy, the tension palpable. It was raining cats and dogs, as we say, back home. To be honest, we were all on edge. Some, silent, were already elsewhere in their minds. In just two hours, we would be parachuting into Normandy, and while we were proud to participate in this much-anticipated 'DDAY,' fear gnawed at our stomachs. The sergeant, aware of the anxiety gradually gripping his men, called out to me :

— Peter Gordon, you always have a harmonica with you, haven't you ? Play us something.

I straightened up and, without a word, took my harmonica out of my 'Denison Smock' jacket pocket to start a respectful 'God Save the King,' but the sergeant interrupted me immediately :

— Oh no, may His Majesty forgive me, but don't you have something more 'upbeat' ? Some jazz, maybe ?

Surprised, I remember opting for 'In the Mood.' The effect on my comrades was immediate : their faces relaxed ; they breathed a little easier. Some even tapped their feet to the beat, albeit with slightly forced smiles. Later, I would have the chance to tell Glenn Miller how his music had lifted the spirits of the crew before the big jump. It touched him deeply. Finally, we took off. The weather, which had been atrocious for the past two days, promised a turbulent flight. The night before, a severe storm had hit southern England, making any take-off impossible. This night was to be 'the one', and we felt almost relieved when we were called. To finally act and no longer wait. We were fed up with the war and ready to do anything to end it. In the meantime, the turbulence rocked the fuselage. Outside, the elements were raging. We clung to our seats, and it's safe to say that bravery was the last thing on our minds. We thought of our mothers, our wives, our girlfriends, to avoid thinking about what awaited us below.

*

At the sergeant's request, Peter Gordon had resumed playing his harmonica. Unfortunately, it was futile. The infernal noise of the fuselage, which seemed to be falling apart, drowned out the music. Nevertheless,

Peter Gordon was flattered that he had been asked. He didn't know that Sergeant Smith knew about his love for music and that he always carried a harmonica. He couldn't say why, but it pleased him. After the war, if they survived, he would talk about it with him. When all this was just a memory. For a moment, he thought of Ruby. The two friends had promised to meet again later. He would return soon. It was different now ; someone was waiting for him. He thought about their last goodbye, a few days earlier. She was ironing.

— Where are you going to ? No, of course, you can't tell me. What does it matter anyway ? But you have to promise me you'll come back soon. Okay ?

Of course, he had promised. What else could he do ? He tried to catch her eye, but she kept her head obstinately down, focused on that piece of cloth as if her entire life depended on it. She didn't want him to see her cry. She would have plenty of time for that later.

— Did you bring your clarinet ? She finally asked

after noticing the case on the coffee table.

— Yes, I wanted to ask you to keep it. It's a bit cumbersome, and besides, where I'm going, I won't have any use for it. And this way, I'll have to come back, he added, with a somewhat forced smile.

Ruby tenderly caressed his cheek. She slipped away for a moment and soon returned with one hand behind her back.

— Here, this is for you. Don't forget to come back, and take care of yourself.

It was a medallion he had often seen around his friend's neck. The only gift from her mother, who had hidden it in her basket before leaving her on the steps of the Walsall Orphanage, the name Ruby inscribed on it.

— It protected me ; it will do the same for you.

They had kissed briefly, and Ruby had pushed him out the door before breaking down in tears.

*

The old man continued his story. Léo, now silent, never took his eyes off him. He imagined his old friend and his comrades and couldn't help but shiver. Although he had known Peter forever, he had never thought he might have 'fought in the war'. Of course, he was used to meeting veterans, and Colette had taken him to visit the Caen Memorial. But this was different. Tonight, it was as if History itself had entered the small parlour of the Hôtel de l'Aiguille. A wave of tenderness overwhelmed the young boy, and he took the old man's hand. But Peter was far away, and his hand tightened.

— The red light started flashing. It was 1 o'clock, and it was time to jump. We prepared ourselves. One last check, tape on the frames of glasses : we were approaching the drop zone. There we were. It was time.

Léo hung on each of the veteran's words. He seemed to hold his breath.

— Were you scared when you jumped ?

— Of course I was scared ! Jumping into the darkness when you don't know what's waiting for you below is far from reassuring ! But I had no choice. The "die was cast", as we say.

— And where did you land ?

Colette ran her hand through her brother's hair.

— Leave Mr. Gordon alone with your questions !

The young woman, very emotional, was also worried. Would this dive into their old friend's memories prove too painful ? But Peter Gordon smiled at her.

— No problem, I'm actually happy to talk about it. I don't often get the chance to discuss these things. In fact, strangely, I think it even helps me.

He continued :

— I landed in a forest. I stayed hidden there for two days. I managed to detach my parachute, but I was injured. I had a nasty wound on my thigh, and I had sprained my ankle.

He recounted his story. It was as if each memory called forth another. The film played in his mind.

He spoke for himself, for his audience, but also for his dear ghosts, whom he was ready to release, and from whom he was ready to be released... as well. Talking about them was giving them existence again.

Chapter 6

Grand-Bourg-Lès-Essarts, June 8, 1944

Sitting at the end of the table, with his bowl of milk, the child stared fixedly ahead, fascinated. A desperate struggle was unfolding before his eyes : a still-buzzing, but doomed fly, its legs trapped on a sticky yellow paper, was trying to free itself from its snare. Several of these spirals hung from the ceiling. Their dull, continuous buzzing added to the relentless ticking of the comptoise clock that punctuated the silences of the house.

Behind him, indifferent to the insect's slow agony, his mother was bustling about. Running a farm demanded work, even in wartime. A wells-tocked rabbit hutch, a dozen chickens, an old rooster, a few ducks to feed, eggs to collect, milking the only cow, the scarce peelings for the pig, not to mention housework and mending clothes : she had no time to lose. Then, she would have to fetch wood from the shed. Her husband had cut it the day before. For the moment, from listening to the BBC messages, he had 'disappeared'. What Jeanne didn't know was that her husband was an active member of the local resistance network. She often found herself alone running this small enterprise of a farm and certainly had no time. No time to be tender, much less to pity herself.

The farm... It had been different before. Jeanne Groult and her husband Camille were known throughout the region : horse breeders, they also had a cattle herd they could be proud of. In the heart of the Pays d'Auge, on the edge of a beautiful forest, not far from Honfleur, the Buisson Fleuri farm – that was its name – which Jeanne had inherited from her parents, enjoyed a fine reputation. Of course, the war had changed things. The horses had been requisitioned by the occupiers, but the couple had managed to save Gertrude, the cow, and Césarine, the sow, who had to be hidden to avoid being seized. To do this, Camille had set up a space in the back kitchen. That's where they hid her whenever there was 'activity.'

Once she was done with the animals, she would take care of Léontine, her mother-in-law. Now ninety years old, Léontine could no longer see and moved with increasing difficulty. They had set up her chair, a true throne of wicker, padded with old cushions to 'prop her up,' near the small window.

The old woman could then enjoy the warmth of the sun. From her spot, she could still participate in some household tasks like peeling potatoes, carrots, or apples, sorting chestnuts, folding dishcloths. Mother-in-law and daughterin-law didn't talk much. No. But it wasn't a problem. They had nothing to say to each other, that was all. After her husband's death, Léontine had eventually resigned herself to moving in with her daughter-in-law and Camille. It had happened naturally ; she couldn't stay alone, and at that time, a retirement home was out of the question. The elderly had their place in families. So, she had brought a few sheets, her goose down comforters, her chair, a Norman wardrobe, Raymond's old rifle, two hens, and Césarine, the sow. Thanks to their garden, they didn't suffer too much from shortages, and ration tickets allowed them to get bread, sugar substitute, and coffee. They even tried planting tobacco for Camille. Finally, once a week, they made the, *panade*, a bread soup with what little leftover hard bread they had. This recipe was a souvenir from the Great War that the grandmother had passed down to her daughter-in-law. They cooked the bread for a long time in the water. The resulting mush, rich in starch, helped fill the hungriest stomachs.

As for, he had the task of collecting his father's old cigarette butts. He had also learned to make cigarettes with dried sunflower leaves rolled in newspapers.

Grandmother and grandson shared the same room. They got along well, and in the evenings, their laughter could be heard. She called him Fanfan the Fly or just The Fly. He got this nickname from a small brown birthmark on his left cheek. She often told him he had a girl's skin, soft and diaphanous. Which François didn't like at all. Just as he hated the yellow spirals, those cruel and deadly fly traps.

*

A bark soon pulled the child from his contemplation. It was Lucien, the family dog, once again going after the rooster. He loved chasing it but had learned to beware of its spurs over time. Lucien, a deformation of *le chien* (the dog) and also because he resembled a great-uncle of the same name. Like him, he had the peculiarity of being cross-eyed. When, on the day the boy had brought him home to the farm, he described him to the grandmother, she had laughed and exclaimed : 'He's like my brother Lucien.' And so, the name stuck. He was a good dog, an improbable mix of long-haired dachshund and fox terrier. A 'hunter,' as they said on the farm. And it was true that he was unmatched at bringing back all sorts of birds and other rodents which he laid at his young master's feet. François had found him roaming the path behind the pond. Skinny, with a bloody muzzle, he was limping– courtesy of a badger, he supposed. Naturally, he had brought him back to the farm. His parents accepted him on the condition that he stayed in the yard. The boy then made him a kennel big enough for both of them. And it often happened that he would sneak out of his room in the middle of the night, when the house was asleep, to join him. Léontine had eventually discovered his secret but said nothing. Thus, the little boy would return to the house at dawn, before everyone else woke up.

For now, Lucien was calling his master : it was time for their walk in the forest. In the midst of the invasion, it was not safe, and the boy promised not to go far. Besides, he never ventured too far, always fearing he might not find his family when he returned. He knew that innocent people were being arrested, that the war didn't only threaten soldiers. They had come for Francis's father, a classmate, one morning at dawn. It had happened right across from their house, on the other side of the road. A black car had stopped in front of their door. The mayor was there too. They didn't even give him time to dress. Fanfan had seen it all : the mayor in his pyjamas and slippers, the man being arrested roughly, despite his wife's pleas and little Francis's tears. The dog, trying to protect them, had been coldly shot in front of the boy's eyes. That was it. François had seen it all, and since then, going to school terrified him. Yet, he liked André Desmarais, the teacher, and especially Emily, his young English wife.

Fanfan stood up, placed his bowl in the small sink, and put on a vest knitted for him by his grandmother. He gave his mother a quick peck on the cheek as she offered it mechanically, then he left. Not a word was exchanged. That was Fanfan, the Fly ; he wasn't much of a talker. He only spoke to his grandmother and his dog. Today, some might be tempted to find complicated words to explain this refusal to communicate, but back then, people just said, 'François isn't talkative.' And that was enough.

In the yard, the two companions played for a bit, delighting in their reunion. Today, the boy's mission was to pick elderflowers. Infused in water for a few days with sugar and lemon, when they could get it, it made a delicious drink he loved. He called it 'champagne' because it fizzed. Later, with the berries, Jeanne would make syrup that would treat the whole family during the winter. She often said that elderberries cured everything, from coughs to fevers, and even relieved Grandmother's rheumatism.

To be honest, what François loved most was feeling 'important'. For a few hours, he wasn't 'little François,' the boy who went unnoticed, but the one who would help them feasts and heal because, truth be told, at home, it was all about Marcel, his older brother. Marcel, the brave, the courageous one, who hadn't hesitated to join the Resistance : the family's pride. Later, he would be 'Marcel the victim,' the one for whom their mother would tremble, whose photo would sit on the sideboard in the living room. The one they would wait for and who, ultimately, wouldn't come back ; Marcel the hero.

In fact, François knew the whole story : his brother was in love with Emily, but she had ignored his advances. Yes, Marcel, the rejected lover, had acted mostly out of spite. But of course, that wasn't to be spoken of. Naturally, Jeanne understood what was happening and had come to hate the young woman. She felt it deep in her motherly gut : it was 'the Englishwoman's' fault that he had left. Jeanne loved Fanfan, her second son.

She loved him but didn't really see him, and especially didn't show it.

Obviously, he didn't have Marcel's stature. He was a pale, sickly boy with knobby knees and a perpetually runny nose. He was afraid of the war, terrified that it would catch up to him. Marcel was a hero, and François, in his shadow, trembled. The only place where he wasn't afraid was in Lucien's kennel.

A strange boy, indeed, who found his sense of existence in the hares, crayfish caught in the stream, eels sometimes, mushrooms in autumn, and everything the forest offered to those who knew it well. He also helped his father when they went set out to distil the apple juice to obtain the precious Calvados. The two would leave for the day, going from farm to farm. They were called upon to distil raw cider. A travelling distiller, Camille had made a name for himself in the close-knit world of small-scale distillers and was in high demand.

In autumn, they harvested apples. They cleaned them and crushed them. Then came the pressing stage to extract the juice, which was left to ferment. This juice was stored for several months in vats, and when the good weather returned, they called on Camille Groult. Sometimes, the heady smell of apple brandy floated in the air. They knew then that Camille had been by with his still.

François liked helping his father, even if sometimes the smell of the calvados coming out of the copper pipes made him a bit dizzy. One day, he would always remember, he came home completely drunk. He had tried to 'prime' the siphon and ended up swallowing a good gulp of 70° proof alcohol. The poor boy nearly choked, turning scarlet. They returned to the farm with Fanfan giggling foolishly and Camille vaguely worried. The concern was justified, as what had amused Camille had infuriated Jeanne. What would people say if they saw her boy walking around 'sloshed !' 'Those weren't proper manners !' The mother finally put her boy's head under the cold water tap 'to clear his mind' before sending him for a nap.

The grandmother had tried to calm things down – it wasn't that serious – but nothing could soothe Jeanne. The boy and his father kept a low profile, promising it wouldn't happen again.

François adored his father. He could spend hours watching him work on the farm. Camille was a rather secretive but generous man. Stricken with polio as a child, he dragged his stiff leg like a ball and chain. The war hadn't wanted him. However, he couldn't stand any mention of his handicap. As a child, François didn't realise his father's uniqueness. Of course, sometimes he wondered why he hadn't gone when the other children saw their fathers leave one by one. One day, he even fought with Didier, a boy his age who had called Camille a coward. Mr. Desmarais had to separate them. Didier ended up with a black eye and scraped knees, while François came home with a split lip and a big bump on his forehead. He didn't want to explain the reason for the fight to his parents for fear of hurting his father and got away with a stern scolding.

Chapter 7

The boy and his dog, Lulu, set off running toward the forest. Once under the protection of the tall trees, he began to hum. Beside him, the dog leapt, trying to catch the butterflies swirling above their heads. Summer would soon settle in. Yet, François preferred autumn. His forest smelled wonderful during that season.

The two friends took the path to the cabin near the pond. When he was a little boy, the place scared him. Surrounded by alders and hidden from the road by a magnificent weeping willow, it was a mysterious spot. Jeanne had told him that a great-aunt had chosen to drown herself there to escape an arranged marriage. This family tragedy had fuelled his childhood fantasies and haunted his worst nightmares. For years, early in the morning, when the mist floated over the water, he imagined the desperate young woman resolutely walking into the water and could have sworn he heard her moaning. Over time, he learned not to fear the pond. After all, the place had its advantages. No one came there, especially not his mother, who hated it. He decided to build his cabin there. It was where he chose to hide his marble box, just as Jeanne had hidden her jewellery and silverware at the start of the war ; right before his father dug a trench in the backyard to take shelter in case of an emergency… All this had finished by terrifying the child, and it was after this event that he started sleeping with Lucien in his kennel. Only the warmth of the animal could calm his fear.

Camille had helped him build a sturdy shelter. He furnished it with a bed made of branches and ferns. An old blanket, some chipped dishes Jeanne wanted to get rid of before the war, a candle stolen from the pantry, a few matches and a striker, a bottle of cider, the fishing rod he made to catch roach and rudd from what had become 'his' pond, and his traps. He also hid his notebook there, a journal in which he had written some poems, a few texts scribbled at night when they thought he was asleep. The notebook was stored next to his treasure : a book given by Mr. Desmarais. *Le Tour de France par deux enfants*. François loved travelling with Julien and André Volen, the young heroes of this book that their teacher read to them at school. He promised himself to follow in their footsteps when the war was just a bad memory and he was grown up. He would also go to England, which Emily often talked about. That's why he tried to learn the language in secret from his parents.

The two companions were making good progress when Lucien stopped near a bush. He sniffed for a long time, whimpering, and finally barked. François cautiously approached and decided to arm himself with a stick. Bravely, he pushed aside the tangled branches. What creature could be hiding there ? Wild boars ? A sounder had been spotted nearby. For a moment, he regretted venturing far from the family farm.

— Hello. Don't be afraid… My name is Peter. What's your name ? Could you call your dog back, please ? Don't be afraid…

*

Once again, Léo interrupted — Was that you[1] ?

— Léo, since when do you address Mr. Gordon so informally ? Really, that's not how I raised you !

— Let him… Besides, it's a good idea, the informal address… Yes, that was me. I had been hiding there for two days, with a sprained ankle and a nasty wound on my thigh. As I mentioned, my parachute got caught in a tree, and I had to cut the straps. I got hurt in the fall, and frankly, I was starting to lose hope and, most of all, I was starving !

*

Surprised, François whistled for his dog, who quickly lost interest in the stranger. A butterfly had just flown past his nose ; it was much more amusing.

— You don't have to be afraid. I'm Peter. I am

---

1. *Tu* in French, as opposed to the more formal vous

British, he continued, extending his hand. Do you speak English ?

The child took a step back. He had understood. They stood there observing each other, the Englishman trying to gain the child's trust, Fanfan wondering what to do. Jeanne constantly reminded him not to talk to strangers. Especially in wartime when the enemy was everywhere. Despite this, he decided to go against his mother's instructions and shook Peter's hand with great seriousness.

— I'm François.

— Will you help me, François ? I think I've broken my ankle and I've hurt my thigh. I need to hide until I can walk again. I also need something to drink and eat. Do you think you can help me ?

Fanfan "the Fly" nodded. Yes, he would help him. He immediately thought of his secret cabin. No one would find him there. He bent down, offering his shoulder for support. They walked for a good hour. It was difficult : he chose to go through the forest for safety. Peter was heavy, especially burdened with his weapons and cartridge belt. Progress was arduous, and the Englishman grimaced in pain. The boy regretted not having his brother's muscles, which would have allowed him to carry the gear, but at the same time, he couldn't help but feel proud. He too, in his own way, had entered the war.

After helping his charge settle in and closing the door of the cabin as best he could, François headed back to the farm, determined to find some water and food. He would have to be cunning and avoid drawing too much attention to himself to prevent being roped into chores by his mother or father. A crust of bread, leftover soup from the previous day, a bit of butter, some swedes, his canteen filled with tap water ; in the pantry, he grabbed a jar of blackberry jam and a drop of calvados, which he put in a small bottle. Finally, he searched for a tube of ointment to treat the wounded thigh. This ointment was a family recipe, a blend of starch and nettle powder, passed down by Léontine from her grandmother. A bandage, two planks to make a splint, another candle, and he was ready. Before leaving, he went to kiss his grandmother. She had fallen asleep. Gently, he pulled up her blanket over her legs, adjusted her cushions, and softly caressed her cheek. A glance out the window showed his mother coming back towards the house. He couldn't delay ! He quickly set off again. Lucien was already waiting for him at the gate. On the way, he picked up a few cherries that the starlings would have stolen.

— Thank you, boy, you're spoiling me. Thanks to you, I'll recover quickly !

*

The old man paused to pour himself a second glass. A soft, slightly melancholic smile lit up his face.

— I wasn't so bad in my hiding place. François had set up a nice cabin. He was a bit of an unusual boy, but I liked him. Yes, he was a bit like you, Léo, a bit of a loner, a dreamer, spending hours alone on the beach skipping stones... His only friend was his dog, a good creature that followed him everywhere and whom he called Lulu.

— At least he had a dog ! muttered Léo, casting a reproachful look at his sister.

Chapter 8

François made a habit of visiting Peter twice a day. If his mother had paid more attention to him, if only she had looked at him, she would have seen the change. He stood taller. Day by day, the young boy shed his childhood. A young adult was emerging, stronger, prouder too. His gaze became steady, the slight stammer that had made him so unhappy diminished. François grew. Lucien's kennel became increasingly narrow for him, even though he still sought refuge there. The trust Peter had placed in him, the feeling of being useful to someone finally allowed him to step out of his brother Marcel's shadow, whose absence filled the house with silence, taking up all the space.

One morning, as he approached the cabin, he heard music. It had been a few days since Peter had been confined in the cabin, and unfortunately, the supposedly miraculous ointment had not prevented his thigh wound from becoming infected, and his broken ankle still caused him great pain. That day, despite the danger, he had taken out his harmonica. The notes transported him across the Channel, to a small pub with the lovely Ruby. She was there, serving a customer. He imagined her welcoming him with a beer ; her emerald eyes, her pearly smile, and her long legs hidden in wide pants... When you're in pain, when you're scared, it's always good to think of a pretty girl.

François entered the cabin quietly. Peter was sitting on his makeshift bed, his back against the wall of branches. He played with his eyes closed, his head tilted back. The boy, who had already heard this music at Emily's, sat down without saying a word.

*

— Were you there, my friend ? I didn't hear you come in. I was dreaming... I was thinking of my friend Ruby. Do you like this music ? The boy nodded.

— Jazz, he murmured.

— You know jazz ? Do you know how to play the harmonica ? I can teach you if you want... Here, this is for you, he continued, pulling a second instrument from his bag. Music is meant to be shared, take this please. That's for you. I always carry two harmonicas, just in case. Come. Get closer to me. Do you know Glenn Miller ?

*

— How did he come to know jazz ? A boy in Honfleur, during the war... That's rather unexpected.

Colette spoke up.

— Emily introduced him to it. But I'll talk about Emily later if you permit. So, I offered to teach François everything I knew, and he, who didn't like anyone approaching him, let me show him how to hold the instrument properly. That very evening, he was playing the first notes of 'Moonlight Serenade.' He was quite talented and showed a real passion for this music.

'You're a Zazou,' I used to tell him. He didn't really know what a Zazou was, but the idea appealed to him. After all, being a Zazou meant being someone. And then he felt useful. Peter needed to get back to London, but for now, he needed his protector.

Le Buisson fleuri

Jeanne Groult was sitting in the room, peeling vegetables, when she heard the creak of the old gate. It was Robert, the mailman. The mother turned deathly pale and put a trembling hand to her heart, as if to keep it from racing. She stood up, wiped her hands on her apron, trying to compose herself. From the courtyard, sensing her anxiety, Robert gave her a reassuring smile. No need to worry, everything was fine.

It was news from Marcel. The long-awaited, much-hoped-for card had finally arrived after weeks. Marcel, who was not usually sentimental, had poured all his tenderness into sending this reassuring note.

My Dear Mother,

How are you, dear Mum ? Is Dad well ? And Fanfan ? And Grandmother ? Do you get my news regularly ? I am well here and eating my fill. Do not worry about me. Are you still catching cold ? Take good care of yourself, dear Mother. Receive my sweet and affectionate thoughts,

Your loving son,
Marcel

It was one of those yellowish, pre-printed cards, strictly reserved for family correspondence, with little space for personal writing and phrases to be crossed out when not applicable. A smile lit up Jeanne's face and eyes.

Her son was alive ! Of course, the message was brief, but that didn't matter. He was alive, uninjured, and not hungry : what more could she ask for in these troubled times ? Finally, the stamp on the card told her he was in Le Havre. It wasn't far, and that warmed her heart. In peacetime, Marcel loved to stroll on the Honfleur pier and look across the Seine. Yes ! Her son was alive ! That was what mattered ! To hell with the world and the war ! Her mother's heart was now pounding with joy. Yes, her farm was her universe. To those who sometimes criticised her for her lack of engagement, she would say that her country was her family, and if everyone did the same, 'Well, the world would be a better place !' She always ended her tirade by noting that 'it's easy to be De Gaulle when you're hiding in England !' Camille had been tempted to talk to her about the Resistance but had decided against it. For the moment, Jeanne had forgotten the war. She held the card in her hands and, unusually, smiled. She even offered the messenger a rare cup of coffee.

Léontine and Fanfan entered the room, drawn by the noise.

— He's doing well ! Do you hear that, he's doing well !

Of course, the grandmother and the child rejoiced with her, though Fanfan couldn't help but think he had never seen his mother so cheerful. Finally, after kissing the two women and bidding the mailman farewell, he called Lucien and headed for the forest. Peter was waiting for him…

*

Unfortunately, despite the careful attention his protector gave him, Peter's wound was not healing. On the contrary, the infection weakened him more each day, and that morning, the boy found him lying on his pallet, burning with fever and delirious. He had tried to ease his suffering by placing wet cloths on his forehead, but nothing helped. His thigh was increasingly swollen. It was then that François made a significant decision, one of those that turn a child into a man. After covering his friend and gently closing the wooden cabin door, he turned back and walked determinedly towards the village. For a brief moment, he thought about the punishment that would surely follow if his mother found out what he was about to do, but 'in war, as in war', he told himself, he couldn't leave Peter like that. And besides, it was all too much for his child's shoulders. He needed help. But it had to be someone he could trust. Someone who wouldn't betray Peter. The solution was clear : Emily was the only one who could help. She would agree, and she would keep quiet.

Chapter 9

Emily, André, and Marcel

Hired as a nurse by a wealthy family in the Orne region, the young woman arrived in France in the 1930s. A trained nurse, she was enchanted by the idea of living in France for a few years. It was at the Bagnoles-de l'Orne racetrack that she met André Desmarais and Marcel Groult on a warm July evening in 1936. That night, it was mild, and the two friends, leaning against the bar, quickly noticed the young woman, her slender figure, and her thick auburn hair. As usual, they decided to approach her together.

André and Marcel, inseparable friends since school, shared everything. As adults, however, they had taken different paths. André, the calmer and more intellectual of the two, chose to become a teacher, while Marcel, more traditional, dreamed of fields, cows, and horses. He would take over the family farm and modernise it. Against his friend's eccentricity, he posed his down-to-earth common sense. His life, like a furrow in the ground, was straightforward, with no surprises except for the vagaries of the seasons. He would marry and have at least one son to replace him when the time came.

Marcel resembled the land he cherished. With a rugged chin, dark eyes, and a silent demeanour like his mother, he seemed carved from a single block. He had black hair, tanned skin, powerful hands, and broad feet, firmly rooted in the ground. Despite his cavernous voice, it was surprisingly gentle, as was his smile.

His eternal companion was in some ways his negative double… Tall, slender, blond, with an enormous nose, André was a true Zazou. With long hair, extravagant outfits, a Django Reinhardt-style moustache, and always a jazz tune on his lips, he never went unnoticed. He was an eccentric, likeable young man who had 'grown crooked,' as his mother put it.

André, the literary one, often said that he and Marcel were like the oak and the reed. In the village, they were nicknamed Croquignol and Ribouldingue or Laurel and Hardy, so accustomed were people to seeing them together. And, as expected, both friends fell under the spell of the pretty Emily.

She was full of life and loved music. A great admirer of Glenn Miller, she naturally preferred the eccentric André over the down-to-earth Marcel.

Thus, in May 1938, she left Bagnoles-de l'Orne to marry the teacher. Shortly after they moved in, Emily became the assistant to Dr. Nollet, the village doctor.

She didn't have much trouble being accepted by the inhabitants of Grand-Bourg-Lès-Essart, except perhaps by Jeanne Groult, who took it as a personal affront that the young woman had chosen André over her son.

*

The Desmarais couple was very well liked. The young woman, courageous and resourceful, knew how to handle things. She never refused to help, and people often knocked on her door. When they moved into the pretty half-timbered house next to the school, the young woman introduced herself to the notorious neighbour known as 'mother Goulon.' Craftily, she asked her for cooking lessons.

— You see, I'm English, and I would love to learn the secrets of your cuisine… she had simpered.

Lucienne Goulon couldn't resist, flattered that someone sought her out, even though she wasn't a better cook than anyone else. Later, in November 1942, it would be she who knocked on Emily's door : Paulette, her eldest daughter, was in a 'delicate condition' or, to put it plainly, 'embarrassing.' Lucienne and Paulette had hidden the pregnancy, as the future mother's fiancé had been a prisoner in Germany for a year ! Fortunately, the pregnancy went unnoticed, as the young woman remained very slim. Later, when it became impossible to hide Paulette's curves, she stayed hidden in the parental home. One evening, the two women called on their young neighbour, and naturally, young Mrs. Desmarais performed wonders. A baby girl was born, entrusted to the Sisters of Charity, all in the utmost discretion. This secret birth definitively won Lucienne Goulon over to Emily's cause.

André and Emily were passionate about the Zazou movement, their way of combating the dreary grey-green period. Yes, swing was their space of freedom, their oxygen. Certainly, they didn't go unnoticed in the village and were gently mocked. 'The teacher and the Englishwoman' were seen as they were whimsical lovers, slightly eccentric, likeable young people, but ultimately not very serious. Some pointed fingers at them, notably Jeanne, who still resented Emily for not choosing her Marcel. They were sometimes criticised for not getting involved. It was easy to be Zazou, but was it the time for laughter and dance when others were dying ? On November 11, 1940, they participated in the student demonstration at the Arc de Triomphe.

No, being a Zazou wasn't trivial, they defended, it was a way to resist, but without violence. They preferred their umbrella to a weapon, that was all.

And too bad if people didn't understand them ! When they could, they went to the capital to attend clandestine concerts and became regulars at the Gaveau Hall. Together, they attended the first swing festival.

At one of these Parisian concerts, André was arrested during a police raid. Many were taken that night. Emily, by chance, hadn't accompanied him, feeling tired. André and his companions were sent to Drancy. He stayed there a few days 'as an example' before being miraculously released.

Increasingly, they were seen as brats, teenagers who didn't want to grow up and especially who shirked their responsibilities. The collaborators despised them, suspicious of their influence on the youth ; the resistors, who didn't hesitate to 'risk their skins,' weren't far off either. Moreover, contrary to what this fashion implied, jazz wasn't forbidden, even true jazz lovers, the purists, mocked them. Talk to them about Armstrong, Miller, but not Trenet and his *'poule zazou'* !

The 'poule zazou,' as Jeanne had definitively nicknamed Emily. And in her mouth, it wasn't affectionate. When André was arrested, she openly rejoiced. It would teach them a lesson ! When he returned, she made it known that it wasn't 'a heavy price.' But he had nothing to pay, people pointed out. She replied exactly, knowingly. Some took more risks in life, like her Marcel. Emily made André promise not to go to Paris anymore, at least for the duration of the war. He promised.

*

Ne pas subir

The couple organised zazou parties at home. Emily took care of the decorations, using whatever they had on hand. For these evenings, their apartment took on the air of a London pub. She had made a poster. *In the Mood* it read, a nod to Glenn Miller, her idol. On the back of the poster, she had written *Ambiance*, the French translation of the trombonist's title. In case of a police raid, they would simply flip the poster. With censorship tightening, they had to be cautious. Some portraits, a few titles, and of course, their motto 'Ne pas subir' (do not endure) adorned the poster. A cushion in the colours of the Union Jack, two others in American and French flags, were proudly placed on the small couch. On party nights, they covered the windows for more discretion.

No, the Nazis would not steal their youth ! And even if they no longer had grenadine beer, they would drink cider. They danced a lot and, of course, they had to wear eccentric outfits. The girls dressed in bright colours. If they ran out of lipstick, they used beetroot. They wanted to have fun at any cost, to escape the prevailing gloom, not to surrender their youth to the war and the occupiers. And to hell with the curfew, they had overnight parties, 'surprise party overnight'. That became the code name for these gatherings.

Other times, they organised literary evenings. They read excerpts from Aragon, Malraux, or Claudel. They loved Boris Vian's jazz and his commitment, even if they regretted that he did not join the zazous. One day in 1942, André arrived very excited.

— Camus talks about us in *L'Étranger*, his

first novel !

He read aloud : 'a little later, the young people from the suburb, passed by, with slicked-back hair and red ties, with very tight-fitting jackets, with an embroidered pockets and square-toed shoes', and ended with a bow.

But one morning, just as dawn was breaking, there was a knock at their door. Emily turned deathly pale, and silence fell. They had prepared for the possibility of a raid. In the blink of an eye, everything was tidied up. Cushions hidden, posters flipped, photos taken down. After ensuring everything was in order, André, very dignified, went to open the door. It was Pierre, a childhood friend with whom he had got into much mischief. But today, everything separated them, and this visit was not friendly. Pierre had joined the national militia.

— Pierre, what a pleasure to see you, began the Zazou with a bold air…

— Sir Desmarais, we ask you to follow us… It seems you're hosting parties here. Identity checks for everyone !

He pushed André and forced his way in, followed by three of his colleagues. Among them was Jules, another childhood friend. As a child, Jules had been the class's whipping boy, and it was André who had played the role of protector. Yet, without any scruples or gentleness, he shoved the one who had protected him. This new power had something intoxicating for the former humiliated boy : he was taking his revenge. And so what if he had to arrest his guardian angel ! After all, 'He was just following orders.' This phase would later become his leitmotif. 'I was just following orders'... and to hell with if it led others to hell.

— Sir Desmarais, I ask you to get dressed. You will have to come with us.

— I am dressed, I suppose. You don't like my outfit, Pierre ? Do you want one of my jackets ? I can lend you one.

And so, in his zazou outfit, he left, head held high and umbrella in hand.

— See you later, he whispered to Emily with a wink. Don't worry.

But at that time, André did not return. After a stay at the Kommandantur, he was sent to a camp, far from Grand-Bourg. It was discovered that the teacher's plaid jacket was a cover. They returned to search the house. It was in the frame of André's bicycle that they found the documents that would seal his fate. Yes, the teacher was a Zazou, but he was primarily the head of a very active network in the region. 'Being seen, to hide better' was his bet. It worked, for a time. Emily, miraculously, was spared that day. Her status as a nurse saved her : Dr. Nollet needed her.

That was in 1942. It had been two years. An eternity.

Chapter 10

As usual, Emily greeted François with a big smile. They settled in the kitchen, and the young woman prepared him a slice of bread and butter.

— Eat, Fanfan. We'll talk later.

She was like his grandmother ; every time he visited, she would feed him. 'Eat, you don't know who will feed you.' As long as there was food, everything was fine. Emily watched him silently. She waited, thinking that if she ever had the chance to be a mother, she would want a child like him. 'You'll see, things will get better after the war. Anyway, he wouldn't be happy. I want my child to grow up without fear,' André Desmarais would say to reassure her. But it didn't comfort her. So, she had grown attached to François, and a strong bond had developed between them. Sometimes, her gaze turned melancholic, and she shook her head, as if to chase away the sad thoughts that kept her awake more and more often at night.

— Have you heard from Marcel ?

The child nodded, shrugged. Yes, they had just received news.

Everything was fine ; he wasn't there to talk about his brother. The young woman gently apologised. In truth, François was a little jealous of Marcel and Emily. At that precise moment, he was almost glad that his brother was absent because he increasingly cherished these little moments with her. The English lessons and the music she sometimes played for him. André Desmarais found this amusing. 'As long as it's François and not his brother,' he would say, taking her by the waist. 'You stupid thing ! Be careful, though, he'll grow up !' she would invariably reply, laughing.

*

She let him finish his snack, and then he began to reveal his secret. He needed her. Peter was sick, badly injured, and he had not been able to heal him.
— I put Mum's ointment on him and gave him syrup. He's going to die, and it will be my fault. He trusted me.

François started crying. Long, rough sobs choked him, preventing him from speaking further. He began to rock back and forth, a sign of great distress for him, twisting his fingers. Emily approached him. Gently, she wiped his tears, helped him blow his nose, and took his hands in hers.
— Calm down, François. Whom are you talking about ? Who is injured ? I will help you, but first, you have to explain. To do that, you need to calm down.

Her voice was soothing, soft.

— It's Peter. I found him.

The sobs were starting to lessen. I hid him in my cabin. He's like you. He's English. You have to help me, Emily, but you mustn't tell anyone. Or else they will arrest him. Promise me, Emily, that you won't say anything.

Talking about it made him feel better. Shared, the secret became less heavy. He was no longer alone, and Peter would get better. He wouldn't be angry with him for telling Emily. Of course, she would help. She took her nurse's kit.

*

On the way to the forest, she praised him. Who would have thought that Fanfan la Mouche, a bit special, a bit wild too, would be capable of such an action, such bravery ? He was a like her, an outsider among his own. She reassured him, he didn't need to worry, she would take care of his charge. At least, that's what she hoped. When they arrived at the cabin, Peter was unconscious. His forehead was burning.

— Help me, Fanfan, we need to undress him. I have to check his wound.

*

'We'll have to take off his pants. I'll get ones from André. They wear the same size.

She had to be careful. During these troubled times, her accent could be a problem, and even though people knew of her existence, Emily preferred to remain discreet. To some, she would always be 'the Englishwoman'. Since the night of the landing and the 'choke points', these sacrificed cities, there was much resentment towards the allies for bombing civilians, even if it was for the 'good cause.' Jeanne felt this resentment more than anyone. She was furious. Camille had been in Caen that night. He had supplied his sister with cream and butter and stayed to sleep at her place. Later, much later, he would recount waking up in the middle of the night, the flares, the bombs raining down without stopping for hours. His sister disappeared that night ; Camille had just enough time to take shelter before a final bomb completely destroyed the house. 'No need for the "boches" to kill us,' she said to anyone who would listen, 'the allies are taking care of it !'

Emily noticed a metal box that appeared to be Peter's first-aid kit. She opened it. Inside were a pair of scissors, soap, a Velpeau bandage, and some gauze. She had brought morphine, which she kept at home for emergencies, and a syringe. She also had sulfa drugs, which she hoped would stop the infection.

— Damn, I have nothing to disinfect with !

The boy handed her a small bottle :

— Can you use *calva* to disinfect it ?

— Perfect ! He's really lucky to have you, she said, nodding toward the injured man.

They stayed with him all afternoon, monitoring

his temperature and waiting for him to wake up. At 4 PM, he finally opened his eyes and jumped at the sight of Emily.

— Don't be afraid, Peter. This is my friend. Her name is Emily, and she's English like you. She treated you. You were in bad shape, and I couldn't leave you like that. You were going to die.

Emily watched the boy with a smile. She realised she had never heard him talk so much.

— Fanfan, I'll stay with your friend. We have things to discuss. Can you go to my house and get André's pants from his closet ? There's no one at home, you won't risk anything.

François left, leaving them alone. Sharing this heavy secret was a relief, and sharing it with Emily pleased him even more, like a secret bond that united them.

*

When he returned to the cabin, Peter seemed better already. They helped him put on André's pants. A bit too big at the waist, a piece of string served as a makeshift belt. The boy had made a detour by the farm to bring something to eat. A chunk of bread and some butter. He even managed to find a hard-boiled egg. If his mother complained, he would say he was hungry. The important thing was for Peter to recover as quickly as possible.

As he was about to leave the house, his grandmother called him.

— What are you up to, Fanfan ? I've been

watching you these past few days. I'm not completely blind, you know.

— Nothing, Grandmother, he replied, maybe a little too quickly. But please, don't tell Mum you saw me.

Of course, Blanche, his eternal ally, promised.

— Be careful, though. There's 'movement' these days, and it's not too safe to walk alone.

— I have Lucien, don't worry !

The old woman couldn't help but smile. She adored the little one. He reminded her of Camille when he was young. A good boy.

The two accomplices had organised themselves so their charge would lack nothing. She went in the morning, and he visited in the late afternoon, pretending to walk the dog. Soon, Peter got better, and Emily proved to be an effective ally. She was the one who mailed his letters. Finally, it was decided that Peter would be safer at Emily's house, and one night, they braved the darkness and patrols to leave the cabin.

Thanks to the young woman, Peter got in touch with a fisherman who agreed to take him to England. To compensate him and help her compatriot, Emily sacrificed a gold ring brought from England. Her mother had engraved her name inside the ring, the last gift from a mother to a cherished daughter. Touched, Peter promised he would return to buy it back. The bet was risky, but young Peter decided to take his chance. He absolutely had to return to England. They needed him there, and he couldn't continue to expose François and Emily to danger. Thus, with a heavy heart, and after managing to steal a kiss from the pretty nurse, he boarded. The three friends promised to see each other again when all this was over.

The boat departed on a moonless night, a foggy night that would conceal them. The crossing was arduous, the sea turbulent, and they had to avoid the many German patrols. The fisherman and his passenger eventually landed in England, exhausted and completely soaked. 'The harmonica has found its case,' was the coded message Peter made sure to broadcast on the BBC to reassure his rescuers.

*

Peter's voice broke. He apologised and asked to retire. He would continue his story the next day. Of course, Julie Anne would join them. That night, sleep was long in coming to the Hôtel de l'Aiguille. Peter Gordon, tormented by the memories he had just stirred up, tossed and turned in his bed. Eventually, he got up and settled into the worn-out armchair, grabbing a small notebook Colette had placed on the side table for him, and began to draw. It was always the same drawing that had soothed him for fifty years. A face with delicate features, hair styled in bands, deep and dark eyes, and an enigmatic smile, a bit sad too. The young woman now looked at him. She had been accompanying him for so long.

— Good night, Emily, he sighed.

Chapter 11

The next morning, Léo was the first to wake up. His night had been restless, waking up with a start several times. At six o'clock, unable to stay in bed any longer, he entered his sister's room.

— Léo, you really need to stop barging into my room like this… You're not a little boy anymore…

— I couldn't sleep. I have an idea.

He slipped under the duvet. Colette sighed. She knew her brother. Her night was definitely over.

— Come on, tell me…

— I thought about Mr. Gordon's story all night. Do you think 'Fanfan la Mouche' is still alive ? I'm going to look for him. And if we invited him for Christmas with Mr. Gordon ? Wouldn't that be a nice surprise ? And then there's Emily… Do you think she was his fiancée ? Do you think she's alive ?

Colette smiled. Yes, it was a lovely idea. She would think about it. For now, it was time to get up and prepare breakfast. Then she would go knock on the door of room 22.

*

In the morning, she secluded herself in her office. In a notebook, she found Ruby's contact information and called her immediately. Peter Gordon had arrived two days earlier. She had been a little worried to see him alone. Was Ruby well ? Ruby reassured her. Colette then recounted the previous evening's events, Peter's story, and Léo's somewhat crazy idea. Could she tell her more about François and Emily ?

Ruby remained silent for a few moments. She had very rarely heard about Emily. She only knew that she had been deported and hadn't returned. For fifty years, her ghost had haunted Peter. She didn't know much more. As for François, yes, he was still alive. He was growing old on the family farm he had never left. Ruby offered to contact him, but Colette preferred to handle it with Léo ; it was his heartfelt idea. She would get back to Ruby as soon as possible ; Christmas was approaching… Finally, before hanging up, Ruby asked her to take good care of old Peter. She had been worried about him for some time ; he seemed rather 'elsewhere' sometimes. He also needed to remember to take his heart medication ; it was important. Of course, Colette promised. No worries, Léo and she would take care of their favourite guest.

She decided to devote her day to the old man. Truth be told, her conversation with Ruby had moved her. She couldn't help but imagine the old Peter waiting for a young woman who would never return. And Ruby ? She was beginning to understand the strange relationship they had ; the childhood friend, the lifelong companion. How could one compete with a memory ?

*

As the day was beautiful, the three friends went for a walk-in Fécamp. On the pier, facing the sea, they stopped to contemplate 'La femme de pêcheur' facing the sea. Her brother, like most Fécamp residents, called her, because of her position, 'Madame de Cuverville[2].' This nickname always made him laugh. This sculpture had always moved Colette. That solitude and stubbornness, and that need to wait and above all to hope… The old Englishman was like this fisherman's wife. He had waited, hoped, for years. And life had passed by. Wars didn't end on Armistice Day or with the capitulation. Fifty years later, Emily still missed Peter. His entire life had been disrupted, and certainly Ruby's too. Once again, a wave of tenderness overwhelmed the young woman, who couldn't resist hugging the old man.

— Let's go back, Peter.

But he had taken out his harmonica. Soon, the first notes floated away, nostalgic and tender, like a caress. It was the music of lost years, of happiness gone. Colette, moved, hugged Léo. When they left, Léo timidly put his hand in the veteran's,

---

2. Play on words meaning "ass-to-city"

and against all expectations, he took it, trembling. He held on as if to a lifeline.

A surprise awaited them at the hotel. Ruby was there. Sitting at the bar, refreshing herself with an Abbey Ale, 'The best beer there is.' Indeed, she had barely hung up the phone when she decided to join her friends. It had been a long time since she had come, and her conversation with Colette had made her want to see them all again. She was there, dressed in pink, an outfit that her idol, the Queen, could have worn. The reunion was joyful, and Ruby's characteristic laugh soon echoed through the little hotel. She had brought small gifts for her friends : a knitted scarf for 'old Peter,' a crocheted doily for Colette, and a bottle opener with Prince Charles's likeness for Léo.

Finally, she placed a box of fruitcakes she had made herself on the table.

*

Ruby Allister

Like Peter, she grew up in the Walsall Orphanage. One morning, the nuns found a bassinet with a little girl on the doorstep of the establishment. This was quite common at the time. The little girl wore a small chain around her neck with a medallion, the last gift from a probably desperate mother who saw no other option but to entrust her baby to the nuns. Next to the girl's head, there was a simple note : 'Ruby,' a precious name, like a final bond between mother and child. The little girl and Peter quickly became very close : a brother and sister, always ready to get into mischief. They even bore a slight resemblance, with the same unruly hair and slightly wild air. When you saw one, the other wasn't far behind. At seven, they were separated. No matter, Peter and Ruby found a passage through the hedge at the back of the garden. It became their rendezvous point and, whenever possible, their escape route. One day – Ruby loved to tell this story – Peter even dressed as a girl to join her in the refectory. Unfortunately, the ruse was ineffective, and it ended with a severe punishment. The nuns were merciless when it came to discipline. That time, Peter had to kneel for a long time on a square ruler, while Ruby got away with a few lashes of the martinet. They had 'mutilated' quite a few martinets over the years, depriving them of their leather straps !

As they grew older, the thick stone walls became unbearable, and it was with great relief that they eventually left what seemed like hell to them. Many thought 'those two' would end up living together. It was 'written,' but life, or rather the war, separated them. She wanted to seize her life, while Peter became melancholic. He stopped laughing, haunted by painful memories he refused to talk about. Ruby eventually grew tired and decided to move on without him. She tried her hand at painting, got a job in a London art gallery, sang in pubs, and became a TV presenter : she fluttered around.

She had many lovers, both men and women. She wanted to be free. No children ; she hadn't been taught to want to be a mother. 'Growing up in the orphanage didn't help.' She eventually moved to France to live with a friend, an artist.

Peter and Ruby stayed in touch, meeting regularly, often at the Hôtel de l'Aiguille. It was a tender, somewhat nostalgic friendship. Over time, they had come to resemble an old couple.

*

They met again for dinner that evening. As he had done the previous night, Peter Gordon invited Léo and Colette to join them. Both accepted, eager to hear the rest of the story. The meal was cheerful. Peter was in good spirits. They talked about the music lesson he had attended. He had been captivated by Julie Anne's personality and her house on the cliff. But more than anything, he had been impressed by the strength and serenity that emanated from the young woman.

— Peter… would you tell us the rest of the story ?

THIRD PART

Summer 44
Chattanooga choo-choo

Chapter 12

'We didn't come here to set up any musical fashions. We simply came to bring a much-needed touch of home to some guys who have been here a couple of years.'
— Glenn Miller, to George Simon
England, 1944

London, August 1944

After wandering through the streets of London, Peter Gordon finally arrived in front of the pub 'The Red Lion.' In the distance, the planes tore through the sky. The respite would be brief, and the night threatened to be gruelling. He stubbed out his cigarette and then pushed open the heavy entrance door. He was expected : Ruby had arranged to meet him there. She had a surprise for him, and he would not be disappointed, she had insisted. They had reunited two days earlier. The return to London had been eventful. As promised, Peter had been able to reassure his accomplices. Of course, the reunion with Ruby had been warm, even though she had wished for more enthusiasm from her friend. She had thrown her arms around him, relieved. She had had time to measure her fear and anxiety, and it seemed to her that her feelings for her childhood companion were evolving. She decided to attribute Peter's reserve to the war and what he had just experienced. Now that he was back, life could resume its course. In the meantime, she was eager to reveal the surprise she had been preparing for him for two weeks.

He wouldn't regret it, she had insisted three times.

The young woman had managed to get a job at the Red Lion, where people came to forget the war and the bombs for an evening. Protected by its thick walls and heavy doors, it was a place where people loved to gather. Ruby sometimes even sang there. Her rough, raspy voice perfectly complemented the jazz music people came to hear. Why not take a chance ?

She had thought one evening when offered a microphone.

Behind the pub's entrance gate, a staircase descended to the basement. Peter, growing more curious, pushed open a second, even heavier, padded door. Ruby was serving a customer. For a moment, he stood there watching her. The musicians were finishing tuning their instruments. People were getting restless. They were eager to dance and forget the war and its tragedies for an evening. Suddenly, there was a stir. The crowd rose and applauded. Peter, open-mouthed, had to grab onto the counter.

In a gray suit, his hair slicked back, with his famous wire-rimmed glasses perched on his nose, the awaited guest finally made his entrance, greeting the audience. Peter thought he was dreaming : it was Glenn Miller standing before him.

*

Old Peter still had stars in his eyes as he recounted this memory. Léo, for his part, opened his eyes wide…

*

The musician took his trombone out of its case. Soon, the first notes of 'Chattanooga Choo Choo' filled the air. Couples, who had been waiting for this, joined the dance floor. The women were beautiful on this summer evening in 1944, and it was good to be able to abandon oneself in the arms of a man.

The trombonist winked at Ruby, who responded with a wave. Peter could hardly believe it. She knew Glenn Miller… And it was really him, winking at him… She never ceased to surprise him. A man in the room invited the young waitress to dance, and she didn't hesitate. She joined him on the dance floor, spinning and twirling, visibly delighted, the queen of the dance. With rosy cheeks and sparkling eyes, it seemed nothing could stop her. The other couples soon gave them space, surrounding the dance floor and keeping time. Yes, this music was magical, silencing fear and anxiety.

However, Peter saw none of this and had eyes only for the musician.

During the break, slightly out of breath, Ruby returned to the bar and, as usual, brought a drink to the artist. She leaned in to whisper a few words in his ear. Glenn Miller turned his head in Peter's direction. He couldn't help but smile at the young man's intimidated look. Tall, slim, with rebellious red hair, high cheekbones, clear eyes, and a straight, fine nose, Peter Gordon undoubtedly had a good face. Not necessarily handsome, he had that certain something that could make unattractiveness endearing. At that precise moment, he mostly looked like he didn't know what to do with his long arms, and his emotion made him twist his fingers. The musician invited him to his table. Hesitant and very impressed, Peter looked around. Was it really him they were addressing ? Finally, he took his glass and joined him.

— Ruby tells me you're a musician. Clarinet, I believe.

Peter, increasingly nervous, started stammering. Yes, he played the clarinet.

— How about a little demonstration ? The musician added.

— But I don't have my instrument…

— Yes, you do !

Ruby arrived, holding the case. As always, she had thought of everything. She even had his jazz sheet music !

Peter could hardly believe what was happening. He looked at Ruby, who encouraged him with a nod, and then stood up. After taking a deep breath, he began playing the first notes of 'In the Mood.'

— An excellent choice, the trombonist murmured with another wink as the audience started dancing again.

Peter could have played all evening. He thought his heart would burst when Miller stood up to accompany him. The music transported them far away, far from London and its torments, far from the war and the bombs. But unfortunately, the piece ended, and those who weren't dancing stood up to applaud the two musicians. Glenn Miller grabbed Peter's arm and pushed him forward. Instantly, the young man became a bit awkward again, looking for Ruby in the crowd. How could he thank her for this precious moment ?

— Let's sit down. Ruby, could you bring us two whiskies ? Now, Peter, your name is Peter, isn't it ? These are the best whiskies I know ! Glenmorangie, which means 'valley of tranquillity.' It's beautiful, isn't it ? I love its vanilla flavours, mixed with candied citrus, ripe apricot, grilled walnuts and hazelnuts, its creamy texture. It's smooth ; it reminds me of the honey of my childhood, the dates we ate at Christmas… So, Ardberg or Glenmorangie ?

— But I don't know… Whatever you choose… will be fine.

Once again, he looked like a child, blushing,

afraid to admit he knew nothing about it, as if he feared disappointing his idol.

— A Glenmiller then, he added.

The trombonist burst out laughing.

— You mean a Glenmorangie, I suppose ?

Poor Peter wished he could disappear ; he felt so ridiculous. Scarlet, he stammered inaudible apologies. The wire-rimmed glasses, on the other hand, twinkled mischievously.

— You're right, Peter, it's a great choice ! Glenmorangie is a true nectar. A bit of vanilla, a bit floral. Ardberg is more peaty, a bit bitter in the second note. You'll have to taste both if you want to join my band. We have time before the curfew.

Peter was speechless. Had he heard correctly ? Smiling, Glenn Miller continued :

— Let's be serious for a moment. I need a musician. A clarinettist. My clarinettist stayed back home. You play well. Would you like to join us ? Can I count on you ?

Before Peter could stammer anything, the artist raised his glass.

— So let's have a toast, welcome to my band !

'The evening was merry, filled with laughter and music. Never had Peter felt so happy. Glenn Miller was attentive, considerate, clearly moved by the excitement of his new recruit. He thought to himself that he and the lovely Ruby made a peculiar pair. For a moment, he thought of Jonnie and Steven, his children, waiting for him back home.

They were still kids. He couldn't wait to hold them in his arms, along with Helen, their mother. He rose to join Ruby ; he had a favour to ask her. Seriously, the young woman joined the orchestra, taking hold of the microphone. Her warm, sensual voice filled the small hall. Glenn joined her, and together they offered the audience a magnificent "Moonlight Serenade," full of nostalgia and sweetness. Peter couldn't take his eyes off the scene. At the end of the song, the trombonist took the young waitress by the waist and kissed her cheek. It was one of those timeless moments, filled with tenderness and gentleness. Such moments were rare in those times, and one had to know how to appreciate them.

Leaving the pub, he felt like a different man. This evening marked the beginning of his "new life". Yes, gone were the days of misery and loneliness. Now, he had a family. And what a family it was ! He couldn't have dreamed of a better one ! A family and plans swirling in his mind. Yes, once the war was over… nothing could keep him in London anymore, nothing and no one.'

*

— 'I didn't know Glenn Miller was in London.' For the first time, Julie Anne interrupted her new friend.

— 'He arrived a few days earlier aboard the Queen Elizabeth, requisitioned by the army. He had joined the Air Force two years prior, but his eyesight issues obviously grounded him. No matter ; Captain Miller had founded the Glenn Miller Army Air Force Band and was now playing 'for the troops' morale.' At the time of the landing, he decided to be closer to the GIs far from home and settled in London. He even planned to play for them in Paris for Christmas. In the meantime, the war, which dragged on and claimed young lives far from home, needed to end.'

*

For Peter, the months that followed were certainly the happiest of his life. In recent years, he had taken great pride in learning to play the pieces of his idol, which he listened to on the BBC. 'The Glenn Miller sound,' as it was called, and jazz more generally, enchanted him completely. From the first evening, he felt integrated into the orchestra. He arrived with a bouquet of roses in his hand.

— 'You don't plan to propose to me, I hope,' the young waitress had joked, 'I have other things to do !'

— 'Is it for me ?' Glenn Miller had chimed in, a mischievous look on his face once again. 'I have a gift too.'

It was a harmonica. Three letters : AGM, Alton Glenn Miller, and his signature.

— 'I always carry two harmonicas with me. Never forget, music is meant to be shared.'

Peter blushed with emotion. He didn't know what to say and merely stammered heartfelt thanks. For a moment, the musician even thought he might start crying.

They played for the war-wounded, in hospitals, everywhere they could alleviate suffering and soothe the homesickness of those young men so far from home. Peter finally felt useful, so alive. Yet, sometimes, he felt a pang of guilt… Wasn't it indecent to relish life so much when others were dying, sacrificing theirs for everyone's freedom ? He eventually convinced himself that boosting the troops' morale was essential, not forgetting that he had participated in D-Day. He had nearly died there and wouldn't be here without the help of Emily and her young accomplice.

They welcomed the actress-singer Frances Langford and together, they played a spirited 'Chattanooga Choo Choo' to the delight of the soldiers who couldn't take their eyes off the pretty blonde. Some imagined themselves in that little Tennessee station where they were awaited. Yes, they saw themselves on that train finally bringing them home. Soon, on the platform, that person they missed so much… Good heavens ! It felt so good to forget the war for a moment, and how lovely the singer was !

Evenings were devoted to music. Peter seemed to have forgotten the war and the fear ; he lived to the rhythm of the swing. Even the memory of Emily was fading into the background. He would deal with it later, when the war was over. Besides, Emily was going to reunite with her husband, André. He refused to think about all that, about that deep and unspoken jealousy. No, he preferred to think about the music. To be intoxicated by the music. In truth, life had never seemed so beautiful, and he often had that misleading feeling that nothing could happen to him anymore. When they weren't playing, he listened to Glenn talk about his difficult beginnings, his trombone regularly pawned to eat ; he told him about Helen, about that evening when he played with Armstrong, the day of their wedding. One day, he promised, he would introduce him to his wife, and Stephen and Jenny, his children. One day… Peter was in seventh heaven ; these plans were a promise of future happiness, this family, almost like his new family.

One evening, after the pub had just closed, the trombonist suggested they have one last drink. They needed to have a discussion. 'Man to man' he specified, smiling knowingly at Ruby. But first, they were going to drink whisky.

What were Peter's plans when all this was over ? Taken aback, Peter replied that he didn't have any specific plans. One thing was certain : music would accompany him, whatever he did, wherever he went.

— Even in the States ?

Had Peter imagined it, or had Glenn Miller just suggested he follows him to the United States ?

— Even to the States, he replied, trembling. He took a gulp of whisky to steady himself. For a moment, Glenn Miller thought he was about to cry.

— Thank you, sir, he managed to articulate.

— How about calling me Glenn ? It's about time, isn't it ?

— OK, Glenn, he responded, his eyes shining.

Once again, he looked like a child, his emotion so visible. Finally, the trombonist brought up, Ruby. He wondered about their relationship. Would he be ready to leave London, and the young woman ? Ruby would understand, Peter had replied. Then, Glenn Miller told him about his decision to play in Paris for Christmas. Celebrate the long-awaited liberation, with music. It would be a grand celebration. After those terrible years, the world needed to dance. At Christmas, Paris would be the centre of the world. Of course, Peter thought of François, the 'zazou.' François and Emily. Since his return and the message sent by the BBC, it was the perfect opportunity for a reunion.

As for Emily, he would see. Later.

In truth, Emily wasn't that far away. Her smile returned as soon as the music stopped. But she was married. Sometimes, he found himself hoping that André Desmarais would not return. A vague and shameful hope that he hurried to bury deep within himself. He couldn't help but detest this husband…whom he knew nothing about, which made him feel even more guilty. And yet… He knew he would return to Grand-Bourg-Lès-Essart as soon as all this was over. Perhaps she would want to accompany him when he set off again with Glenn Miller's orchestra ?

*

While Peter, lost in his memories, unravelled the thread of his story, Colette watched Ruby out of the corner of her eye. The old lady, very dignified, looked at her friend. A very soft, though sad, smile appeared on her lips. Their eyes met, and Ruby closed hers with a sigh of helplessness. How could she find her place between an idol and a memory ?

— 'Peter, how about spending Christmas with us ? We could invite François. What do you think ? Ruby ? Julie Anne ?'

But the old man declined the invitation. He seemed aged, and above all, terribly tired. Yet, he felt compelled to finish his story. He owed it to himself. As Colette put another log on the fire and offered her guests some herbal tea, Peter resumed the thread of his tale. His voice became painful. Without realising it, he grabbed Colette's hand, squeezing it as if to hold on, like a man about to drown. His hand was trembling. The young woman, worried, covered that hand, worn by the years, with her own. She squeezed it tenderly.

— 'Peter, this can wait until tomorrow, can't it ?'

— 'No, I must finish. Tonight. Tomorrow, I might not have the strength.'

Indeed, the effort was immense. Just as he had done on June 6, 1944, he was preparing to plunge, but this time it was into his memories. Their darkness mirrored that night when he had to jump into the void fifty years earlier. Just as he had done back then before leaping, he took a deep breath.

— On December 14, Glenn gathered us at the Red Lion. He announced that he was leaving the next day to prepare for the concert on site. We would join him in Paris later when everything was ready. He took off the next day, despite his fear of flying, with his friend, Colonel Baessell. It was said later that the pilot was inexperienced, and the weather was dreadful.'

His voice broke, and he finished, his eyes filled with tears.

But nothing would go as planned. The Norseman UC-64A never reached its destination. It crashed into the sea, probably off the coast of Étretat or Fécamp. This disappearance was a tremendous shock in the swing world. As for Peter, he was devastated. Glenn Miller had been somewhat of a father figure whom he had sorely missed during his childhood. The former abandoned child felt orphaned for the first time. And, even though much later, he would discover a jazz that was less 'smooth,' more 'free,' more 'raw,' Glenn Miller would always remain in his heart the paternal hero who played for the kids far from home. He, who had finally found a family within that 'band,' felt as though he had lost everything, especially his initial dreams of fame across the Atlantic. In memory of his friend and their shared ambitions, he decided to abandon his clarinet and dedicate himself to the trombone. Only Ruby remained, solid, strong, faithful.

And then there was Emily…

Chapter 13

Grand-Bourg-Lès-Essart, June 19, 1944

The street is full of life on this morning of June 19. People are gathering to chat. Of course, the DDay landings are at the heart of all discussions. There is finally hope. Yes, the war will soon be over, and those we miss will finally return.

Suddenly, it appears at the top of the street. A black, sinister, menacing, a harbinger of chaos. One can't help but shiver at the sight of it. People retreat into their homes, curtains and doors closing. The street, holding its breath, frozen by fear, slowly empties.

The black car moves closer, slowly. It feels like a scene from an old black-and-white film. The atmosphere is heavy, the anxiety palpable. These cars are all too familiar, omens of misfortune, suffering, and sorrow. People pretend not to see it, but it is all they can see. Believers make the sign of the cross in brief prayer, the superstitious cross their fingers. They entrust themselves to God, to the Devil, they ward off bad luck.

Unperturbed, it takes its time, dangerous, aware of the turmoil it is sowing, savouring the moment. Predatory, confident in its power, in its strength, it knows its prey is there. It knows the outcome, there's no need to hurry. People tremble at its approach, and dare to breathe after it passes. Relief mixed with curiosity : they want to know.

Who's next ? For whom has it come ? Here, no one has forgotten the arrest of little Francis's father a few months earlier, nor that of the schoolteacher, André Desmarais.

There it stops. 'It's for the Englishwoman,' people murmur in the houses.

The doors open. Two soldiers get out, soon joined by the mayor. Behind her window, Old Mother Goulon witnesses the scene. Emily is at the back of her garden ; she must be warned ! But it's too late. The Germans are already in the yard. It's only a matter of seconds.

There she is.

Lost in her thoughts, 'the Englishwoman' does not immediately see the car or its occupants. These will be her last moments of carefree bliss. She is thinking about André, who will soon return. A few days earlier, she received a letter from him. A card in which he tried to be reassuring, asking her not to worry. He ate almost enough, thought of her every day, and waited to finally hold her in his arms. The letter had taken several weeks to reach her. She had managed to find out that he was detained at Fort de Romainville.

That night, she dreamed a dream : it was all over, André had returned. They were expecting their first child, life could resume. It was a day of celebration in Grand-Bourg-Lès-Essart. François was there, Peter too. Glenn Miller played and they danced.

This morning, she awoke, all smiles, with a deep conviction in her heart that the nightmare was nearing its end. Thus, she decided to do some gardening. Around her, the newly flowered beds, the blood-red poppies in the old stone wall, the primroses like so many splashes of colour scattered in the tender green of the lawn. Yes, life was there, ready to burst forth in a thousand colours, a thousand joys.

But then, she looked up…

Later, Mother Goulon would ceaselessly recount the scene that followed. The brutal arrest, the twisted arm, Emily's silent scream, her gaze, the mayor's pallor, his helplessness, the house ransacked, the jewels stolen, the photos torn, and finally, the flowerbed crushed under the barbaric and brutal heels.

Was this how it was all meant to end ?

*

Emily's arrest plunged the small village into a stupor. People didn't really understand. Sure, she was English, and yes, the 'boches' had been nervous lately. So, tongues began to wag. As expected, Jeanne Groult was the most vehement. 'After all, where there's smoke, there's fire,' she repeated to anyone who would listen. And even though no one knew anything for sure, everyone had an opinion about everything. It was known, for instance, that a fisherman had been arrested a few days earlier. Naturally, people linked the two events.

Only François understood. Terror had gripped him then. He expected the black car to stop in front of their house any day. They would come for him. Maybe they would even kill Lulu, like they had killed Francis's dog... Terrified, he couldn't sleep, jumping at the slightest sound of an engine.

When he finally managed to fall asleep, he was awakened by nightmares in which Emily and Peter were being tormented.

Because yes, it was all his fault. He was the one who had introduced Emily to Peter. He was the one who had put them in contact.

— 'What's wrong, my Fanfan ?'

His grandmother took the boy's hands in hers :

— 'I can see you're not doing well. I hear you crying at night. I hear your screams, your nightmares. And you don't laugh with Lulu anymore. You know you can talk to me. I'm your grandmother. Is it Emily's arrest ? I know you care about her a lot.'

— 'It's my fault,' he sighed, in tears.

Awkwardly, the old woman took him in her arms. She could feel the accelerated beating of her grandson's heart.

— 'What are you saying ? Tell me, I'll help you. I'm here.'

So the boy told her. About Peter, the cabin, the injury, the decision to confide in Emily, Peter's departure, and finally, the two arrests. Then, the immense, consuming fear. The fear of being arrested, the fear that they would kill his dog.

— 'Don't worry, Fanfan, I told you, I'm here. Nothing will happen to you. You're safe. Know that I am infinitely proud of you. What you did was good. A true Resistance fighter. Don't be afraid, the war will be over soon, and everything will be back to normal. Emily will come back, and so will Marcel and André. In the meantime, I want you to stay at the farm. And above all, don't tell anyone about this. Do you hear me, no one. It must be our secret. I hope there's nothing left in the cabin.'

No, Emily and he had emptied it. There was no trace left of the paratrooper's presence. As always, talking to his grandmother calmed the boy. Everything would be fine since she had promised him. As for the old woman, she was overflowing with tenderness and pride for the 'little one.' The boy was gone ; it was a young man who now slept near her. And so, in the silence of the night, she decided that if trouble came, if the black car stopped in front of their house, it would be she who would leave in his place. She would certainly not let them take François away.

Chapter 14

Pension Les Sources, 1994

Peter had declined Colette's invitation to spend Christmas in Étretat. After all the emotions and plunging into his memories, he needed calm and solitude. A few weeks later, they all gathered at the retirement home Les Sources. Julie Anne and Peter had planned to put on a small concert for the residents, while François had been invited and offered to host the group of friends.

For now, everything was happening in the small lounge of the boarding house. Madame Martin was also present.

— 'Mr. Gordon, I have a question for you. Of course, you are not obliged to answer. But I must admit, I'm intrigued. Why were you so insistent on moving into apartment 22 ?'

— 'Yes, I will answer you.'

He looked at François. The two men exchanged a somewhat forced smile. François spoke first :

— 'If you don't mind, Peter, I will help explain.'

He continued. A long time ago, before the war,

this house belonged to the local school. It was where the teacher, André Desmarais, and his wife, Emily, lived. It was also where they were both arrested, two years apart.

Peter then took the floor :

— 'Apartment 22 corresponds exactly to the place where Emily hid me for a few days. Curiously, I believe it is a place where I was truly happy. We had faith in the future, and we were so young.'

Then he stood up.

— 'Follow me.'

He opened the door to his apartment. François was the first to enter. His steps were hesitant : entering this room was like becoming Fanfan la Mouche again. He saw himself as a child, eating his toast, talking with Emily, his friend. He thought of André Desmarais, his teacher ; it was in this same room that he had given him his precious book. Ruby, meanwhile, remained at the entrance, as if petrified. Entering this room meant entering Emily's space. An Emily she had hated as much as she had pitied ; who had stolen those years she had promised to live with her childhood companion. In disappearing, Emily had become untouchable, irreplaceable, and Peter, forever inaccessible. Here, she felt Emily's presence. Yes, Emily was there, everywhere ; in that slightly worn armchair, near the marble fireplace. Wasn't it her making the curtain tremble at the window ?

Peter led them to his bedroom, a spacious room with a window overlooking the garden. Just like back then, one could hear the crystal-clear stream. Of course, there had been many changes. The school and the main shops had disappeared, but the half-timbered house remained intact. Gradually, the heart of the village had become the 'Les Sources' boarding house.

In the middle of the ceiling was a large oak beam, worn by the years. Peter had insisted it remained untouched. The owner had promised. He fetched a chair, asked Leo to help him. He climbed onto it and, to everyone's surprise, retrieved a piece of paper wedged between the beam and the wall.

He unfolded it. It was a drawing. A face. The one had redrawn all these years.

— 'May I introduce you to Emily. This drawing has been waiting for me for 50 years. It's our reunion in a way. I drew it before I left. It was our last evening together. I was the one who hid it here.'

Thus, all these years, he had never stopped redrawing it, to never forget. It was his way of talking to young Emily. This dialogue, which wasn't really a dialogue, had never ceased. He caressed the face on the paper with a smile.

There, he had returned. Ruby, who had for a moment considered joining him at Les Sources, understood that she would never truly belong there. The boarding house would forever remain 'Emily's house.' With a heavy heart, but full of tenderness, she descended to the garden. She needed to breathe, to feel the sun's rays on her skin.

The evening that followed, dedicated to music,

was a pleasant one. They sang and laughed a lot. Some danced. The residents enjoyed themselves immensely. For the occasion, Madame Martin even offered champagne. It wasn't every day they had a celebration ! They parted the next day, determined to see each other again soon.

'In Coutances, they have "Jazz under the Apple Trees," we'll have "Swing by the Stream,"' she said, laughing.

Chapter 15

Ferme du Buisson fleuri, 1994

A Few Months Later

The Buisson Fleuri farm lived up to its name. After a harsh winter, it was an explosion of life, a true firework display of colours : clusters of primroses, carpets of daffodils and narcissus, and other daisies delighted the heart. The cherry tree, white with promises, reigned in the yard, robins responded to sparrows, and swallows danced in the sky. The air was mild, filled with the scents of renewal.

François had taken over the family farm and had never left it. A fire had destroyed part of the house, so he had to undertake some work, transforming the old barn into a lovely little home. He had established his 'quarters' there, even though he continued to live in the main building, which he had modernised. However, he had kept his grandmother's old armchair, as she had passed away in January 1945, a particularly cold winter that claimed many lives in an already weakened population. In the back of the garden, near the chicken coop, was the old doghouse ; the one where he had joined his dog for many nights. He could never bring himself to get rid of it and had stored it there, not too far away. The cabin, however, had long been gone. It was struck by lightning during a storm. But the pond was still there, with its frogs that continued to croak in the summer. It was there that he had buried his dog, Lulu, one autumn day. Camille and Jeanne Groult had passed away almost at the same time. The mother had never recovered from Marcel's death. She hung onto her sorrow and resentment, trying to drown it in anything she could drink. She resented the whole world, Camille for surviving the war, François for still being there, the Englishwoman whom she hoped was dead… It was precisely in the pond that she was found. The accident theory was accepted, although it was whispered at the time that Jeanne had been having very dark thoughts lately. With this second drowning, the pond was forever cursed. Camille, meanwhile, fell ill shortly after.

François was left alone on this farm, which no longer looked much like the one from his childhood. As he aged, he increasingly resembled his father, greying, slightly hunched, stocky. In truth, he hadn't really seen life pass by. The life of a farmer requires many sacrifices, and going on holiday isn't easy when you raise animals. Later, he decided to transform the farm into a guesthouse, which was fashionable. This allowed him to make ends meet, but also, and especially, to meet people.

On the mantelpiece were two photos : one of his grandmother, and a photo of him as a child, with brave Lucien. They had been his two companions, his two allies. Near the photos was a drawing. It was a boat, drawn in black ink on a now-yellowed sheet of paper. He had done it as a child for Mother's Day. For a long time, it had taken pride of place on the family sideboard. And then, his mother had ended up storing it away, replacing it with a poem written by Marcel. François had swallowed his anger and especially his grief, saving his drawing, which, undoubtedly, would have ended up in the fireplace, by hiding it in his cabin. Many years later, he had given it back its initial place, on the sideboard. On the shelf above the armchair was 'Le Tour de France par Deux Enfants.' He reread it regularly, never failing to get emotional upon finding the little note his teacher had written inside. Of course, thinking of André meant thinking of Emily. And indeed, it was Emily he was about to talk about today with old Peter. It was not going to be easy. They had met again with much emotion a few weeks earlier. Of course, Peter had returned once before, at the end of the war. François had then informed him of Emily's arrest and deportation. Neither she, nor her husband André, nor Marcel the older brother had returned. In the end, both the oak and the reed had broken simultaneously. Marcel had disappeared under the Allied bombings in Le Havre in September 1944. André had been executed 'as an example' ; as for Emily, it was learned that she had been deported.

Today, fifty years later, the two were meeting once again. To tell the truth, François hadn't told Peter everything. It was after lunch that he decided to 'come clean' :

— 'Peter, I need to talk to you. I have a confession to make. Please, do not interrupt me. This is not easy. I will answer your questions afterward.'

Peter, troubled, promised.

— 'It's about Emily. At the time, I didn't tell you everything…'

Old Peter suddenly felt his throat tighten. His hand trembled as he brought his coffee cup to his lips. The gesture stopped, suspended.

— 'Emily came back.'

Had Peter heard correctly ? François feared he would interrupt him :

— 'No, Peter, please let me continue. This is not easy. It was in 1946, on August 17 to be exact. I remember it as if it were yesterday…'

Chapter 16

Grand-Bourg-Lès-Essarts, August 17, 1946

It's a market day. Like in all villages, this gathering is important, and Grand-Bourg's market is well known. Situated on the main square, not far from the town hall, people love to meet here : there are benches for the elderly, shaded by the lime tree. The terrace of the only shop is always full.

It's where you buy your newspaper, the bottle of oil you need, Gitanes or Gauloises cigarettes, a baguette when the bakery is closed. During the war, they printed leaflets in the cellar, and hid weapons there too. One evening, during a secret meeting, the police raided the shop. It was a little before the D-Day landings. René, the owner, had just enough time to cover the trapdoor leading to the hideout with an old carpet. After a thorough search, they told him he was suspected of black-market activities.

— 'Why, are you interested ?' the owner had replied.

They left as they came, not without muttering some threats.

Today, people gather, share stories, and continue to heal their wounds. They talk about those who haven't returned, those they still wait for, and about life, which, despite everything, slowly resumes.

The stalls begin to fill, though still meagerly. François has been sent by his mother to sell some vegetables and eggs from the farm. You can also get some homemade brandy, made by Camille. During the war, Calvados from the Pays d'Auge was given the official label protecting its name and origin. This prevented the requisition of the copper stills and the alcohol. With the Armistice, Camille could finally resume his activity as a distiller.

In truth, he never really stopped and used it to serve the Resistance. Like André Desmarais, who hid documents in his bicycle frame, Camille used the pipes of his still.

It's a beautiful morning. Some children play at the washhouse while their mothers take advantage of the sunshine to do their laundry. As always, conversations flow rapidly, in rhythm with the beating of the laundry Once again, they talk about Madame L.'s daughter, suspected of 'horizontal collaboration,' as the expression goes. She had endured the humiliation of public shaving a few months earlier. Few had defended her at the time. Mother Goulon's daughter timidly says, 'Not All Germans were bad.' She is shot a glare. A voice is raised :

— 'You would know, wouldn't you ?'

She is about to respond when a silhouette

appears at the end of the street.

The figure walks hesitantly. A woman ? The hunched silhouette leans on a makeshift walking stick. It's as if time has stopped. A heavy silence suffocates the market's activity. Only the fountain can still be heard. At the washhouse, the women have stopped beating the laundry, the children have stopped playing. They watch her approach. Hearts tighten, some beat rapidly. The scene is reminiscent of the appearance of the sinister black Citroën a few years earlier. Who is it ? It's hard to make out. In this post-war period, people still hope for the return of those who are missing. And as long as there is no official, undeniable proof that the awaited person won't return, hope persists. Against all odds.

The appearance has something supernatural about it. For a moment, she falters, but then straightens up, unwavering. Nothing seems to be able to stop her.

François is the first to react and leaves his stall to run towards her. Marcel ? Jeanne Groult removes her apron, a smile beginning to form on her lips. Then they recognise her.

It's the Englishwoman, it's Emily. The boy wraps an arm around his friend's waist to support her.

— 'You've grown, Fanfan. You're a man now. I'm so happy to see you again…'

But François doesn't have time to respond. A scream tears through the village, filled with pain, anger, and sorrow. It's Jeanne Groult. She has witnessed the scene. She is pale.

— 'What are you doing here ? How dare you ? Why aren't you dead ? Get out of here, Englishwoman ! You have no place here ! You've caused enough harm, you and your kind ! Wasn't it enough to kill my Marcel ? You bitch !'

Jeanne is unrecognisable, her face twisted with hatred.

— 'It's because of you that he left ! And it's your kind who killed him ! And it's your degenerate music that lost your husband ! Get out, I tell you, or I'll kick you out myself ! And the rest of you… Are you going to let her stay ?'

She now addresses the crowd, hands on her hips. Her eyes burn with anger, her mouth twists with hatred and sorrow.

— 'François ! Come here, I forbid you to go near that bitch ! She killed your brother ! Isn't that enough for you ?'

Emily gently pushed the boy away.

— 'Go on, Fanfan, don't worry about me. I have to go to the town hall, they're expecting me.'

She smiled at him. Her emaciated, prematurely aged face retained the softness that François loved so much, the very softness his mother had always cruelly lacked. Her hand trembled, her once beautiful and thick hair had turned gray. Only her eyes retained their sparkle, that spark of life that had charmed Marcel and André back then. Her look and her accent. But all that seemed far away now. So the almost young man turned. He looked his mother straight in the eyes, then he took Emily in his arms and embraced her in a long hug that never seemed to end.

— Thank you, François,' she said, gently pushing him away. 'Go now. Thank you for holding me. It did me good.'

He returned to his stall, head held high but heart-broken. Jeanne Groult grabbed his arm.

— 'Come here ! I forbid you to talk to that Englishwoman. Do you hear ?'

Her Marcel had died under an allied bombing raid in Le Havre on the night of September 9, 1944. That night, more than three hundred planes had dropped their bombs on the port city, literally flattening the city centre.

— 'The bitch ! She must have slept her way out. Come here, I'm sure she gave you lice and fleas ! The mangy one ! Come here, Fanfan, I'll wash you in vinegar to kill the vermin !'

— 'Stop, Jeanne ! That's enough !'

It was Mother Goulon who had left the wash-house to intervene.

— 'What's it to you ? Are you on the Englishwoman's side ? Well, that doesn't surprise me ! By the way, you never told us ? Who was the father of your daughter's child ? Surely not her husband ! He had been gone for a long time ! Of course, you defend her, it's the whore who helped her give birth !'

Nothing seemed to be able to stop her. She was now spewing a torrent of insults. Jeanne was vomiting her anger, her suffering, her rebellion, her years of disappointed hope, this wound that would never heal. How could Emily dare to live when Marcel had not returned ? It was as if the Englishwoman had spread misfortune in the village, as if Marcel were dying a second time.

*

— 'Emily... Emily came back ?'

His voice was pale, his complexion ashen. Peter couldn't contain the trembling that had taken hold of him.

— 'Yes, Peter, she came back. At first, she stayed with Mother Goulon. The doctor offered her back her job as his assistant, but she refused. The entire village was under my mother's influence. And to say the least, they were not kind to her. Bicycle tires slashed, laundry stolen, constant insults... Even those who seemed to like her before the war, when they called her 'the teacher's wife,' turned their backs on her. So Emily resigned herself to leaving.'

— 'Do we know where she went ?'

— 'She came to say goodbye. She found me in my cabin, the one you know well. I continued to seek refuge there whenever I could. She told me she couldn't leave without saying goodbye.'

— 'Did she tell you where she was going ?'

— 'Yes, she told me. And she made me swear at the time to keep it a secret. No one was to know. You see, she wanted to 'forget,' or at least try to.

She also wanted to be forgotten.'

— 'But… did you see her again ?'

— 'Yes. She chose to stay in France. I think she was waiting for André to return. André, of course, never did.'

— 'Is she still…'

How difficult it was to ask the question burning on his lips ! His voice began to tremble. A deep breath :

— Is she still… alive ?'

François came to his rescue.

— 'Yes, she is. She made her life about a hundred kilometres from Grand-Bourg. She quickly resumed her work as a nurse and taught English to the local kids. She never remarried, never had children.'

— 'I told her about you. I told her you had moved to Les Sources.'

— 'Tomorrow, I'm having lunch with her. You're welcome to join. She will be delighted to see you again.'

*

Returning to the boarding house was particularly difficult. Peter, deeply affected by François's revelation, was momentarily tempted to cancel the reunion. Fifty years later, did it still make sense ? He found himself feeling, if not anger, then at least strong irritation. How could Emily have hidden her return from him ? Had he been deceived, fooled by a ghost of a woman, he who had put his romantic life on hold ? If he had known, nothing would have been the same. No, she had no right. Perhaps they would have left them together ? Or maybe, freed from Emily, he could have built a family with another woman ? Returning to his room, he retrieved the drawing hidden in the beam. The prospect of this reunion now terrified him. Would they recognise each other ? He had become so old. He wasn't sure he wanted her to see him like this. And her ? Of course, she would have aged too. Would he find in her the smile that had haunted him all these years ? He couldn't help but find it a bit ridiculous. In fact, and even though he didn't want to admit it, Peter was hurt. If Emily hadn't sought to contact him, perhaps it was because their meeting hadn't been as important to her as he had wanted to believe. There was nothing to see in this 'romance' but a few trombone notes they had danced to before he returned to England. Nothing more. The rest had only existed in his mind. But Emily had promised him nothing. Emily had loved André : it was he she had expected.

Finally, he resented François. Why had he revealed Emily's secret to him ? He would have preferred not to know, to continue and end his life as he had lived it. There was something cruel in this revelation. Emily was becoming definitively unreachable. What was he going to do in this apartment 22 ? Lost in memories that weren't really his ? He now questioned his mirror, his old cracked mirror hanging from his chain. 'Old knucklehead, old fool !

You've truly wasted your life, stuck between an idol and a ghost !'

But no ! Blaming Emily was too easy. He was the only one at fault.

His night was filled with confused dreams. The faces of his two friends mingled, transposed, sometimes it was Julie Anne's face that appeared, and finally Colette's. So many women around him ! And to end his life alone, his head filled with memories and regrets… What irony !

He woke up very early. Once again, he was tempted to cancel the reunion. And yet, he knew he had to go. For a moment, he thought of the young man in the Dakota's fuselage, preparing to jump into the night. It was exactly the same fear. The one you feel before being engulfed when you know you can no longer turn back.

Chapter 17

The reunion took place in a small seaside restaurant. When Peter arrived, Emily and François were already seated, chatting cheerfully. From their smiles, one could sense their camaraderie. The old man advanced with great dignity, his hand clenching the knob of his cane. He tried to hide his growing emotion, focusing on his steps and the beating of his heart. He dared not look at the woman waiting for him, seated on the bench.

— Hello Peter.'

Yes, that voice was indeed the one he had heard fifty years earlier in the little cabin by the pond. Perhaps it was less assured, but it hadn't changed. It was Emily's voice. So, slowly, he raised his head.

— 'Hello Emily.'

The reunion was simple. Emily had become an old lady, of course, but one could still find traces of the old Zazou in her : long white hair sweeping her shoulders, a brightly coloured outfit, round, bright orange glasses. She wore mismatched socks and little girl sandals. Finally, to complete her attire, she was accompanied by an old umbrella. No, this woman was certainly not a ghost. On the contrary, she was a radiant woman, a luminous woman that the shadows of the war had not managed to extinguish. Next to her, Peter felt old. He couldn't help but be ashamed of his cane, regretting having brought it. She would take him for what he had indeed become : an old man, consumed by regrets and nostalgia. In retrospect, she reminded him a little of Ruby. Full of extravagance and joy, laughter and smiles, wonderfully... alive. In his drawings, Emily resembled more a Madonna than a sensual and joyful woman. A woman he had idealised, fantasised about. But no, this Emily had loved, these hands must have caressed, this mouth kissed and bitten into life.

They shared stories of the years gone by, the meeting with Glenn Miller. Emily briefly mentioned her arrest and deportation, without lingering on that painful but distant past. What was the point ?

— 'Why didn't you return to Grand-Bourg ? I mean, now...'

— 'Because I have nothing left to do there. Grand-Bourg is part of the past. A past I loved, where I lived lovely moments and more painful ones. But those moments belong to the past. No, I had nothing left to do there. When I officially learned that my dear André would not return, I decided to continue my life elsewhere. It is always a bit dangerous to live in the past, to get bogged down in memories. Only François and Docter. Nollet knew. I had a beautiful life, one I chose against all odds. And you, Peter ? I understand you decided to live in Grand-Bourg ? What a funny idea !'

He felt a bit ridiculous. How could he explain, without revealing too much, that he had chosen to end his days in Emily's old house to retrieve a fifty-year-old drawing ? Then he realised he would give up his studio, it no longer made sense. Strangely, he felt light, finally liberated. Emily being alive, he no longer had to honour her memory because yes, he had felt guilty all his life. It was his fault that she had been arrested. He who prided himself on not having killed anyone in the war was nonetheless haunted by the young woman's arrest. Those blows she had received, it was as if he had given them to her.

They spent the afternoon together. François had chosen to slip away, these two needed to reconnect. They talked about life, music, and the future. Peter wanted to pick up the trombone again. To hell with age and its troubles !

Yes, that was it, he would start playing again and create an association dedicated to swing. When they parted, Peter felt rejuvenated, alive. The next day, he informed *Madame* Martin that he was leaving his apartment at Les Sources.

*

Emily and Peter saw each other several times after that. They couldn't stop sharing their stories. Peter showed his notebook to his friend. She had always been there, near him. She had accompanied him everywhere. For the first time, Emily felt a certain discomfort.

— 'But I never promised you anything, Peter... And then, there was André. You knew that.'

— 'Don't worry, Emily. I understand. In fact, I think I always knew. I thought you had died because of me, you to whom I owed my life. That thought never left me. I think I forbade myself to welcome another woman into my life ; it was only right that it be dedicated to you. Do you understand that ?'

— But you had told me about a young woman waiting for you in London. I remember it very well, even if I have forgotten her name.'

— Poor Ruby... Yes, I think she waited for me, for a while. In fact, she understood as soon as I returned to London, long before I did... At the time, I didn't know you had been arrested. And I hoped we would reunite. After... Yes, I know, there was André. André... The only man I was jealous of. I hated him, I think. And I hated myself too. How could one fear the return of a man who was a prisoner ? So, I felt ashamed. In fact, I think I punished myself all these years. The only one who could have saved me was Glenn Miller. Following him there, joining his troupe... But Glenn died. And I stayed alone. I ended up thinking I was cursed. 'I must be jinxed,' as they say, the one to be avoided at all costs. Only Ruby stayed by my side. She tried to shake me, to make me react. 'We are alive,' she used to say.

So, Ruby finally got tired. She chose to live without me ; she was right. We remained close, she and I, as we always have. But today, I found you again. You are no longer a ghost. You are here. Your look hasn't changed, nor has your smile. I would like you to forgive me.

— I have nothing to forgive you, Peter. What belongs to the war is behind us. Will you introduce me to Ruby ?'

Against all odds, Ruby had been convinced quite easily. Finally, she would meet the one who had disrupted her life. Meeting her would give her a body, demystify her. Emily would no longer be an idea, a ghost, a drawing in a notebook ; no, she would become a reality. She expected nothing in particular from this meeting, convinced that it would not change the course of her life. But in that, she was wrong.

They had arranged to meet on a beach on the Côte de Nacre. A 'neutral' place, conducive to meetings. The sea was beautiful, offering a whole palette of colours to those who contemplated it. It was a serene and calm atmosphere, all in softness.

Peter and Ruby arrived first. They settled in the sand. Ruby, feeling awkward, decided to focus her attention on a group of seagulls bobbing on the gentle waves.

— She certainly knows how to keep people waiting… – She regretted her rather misplaced remark and added – 'Forgive me, Peter, I'm being silly.

Actually, I think I'm just not very comfortable.'

Then a voice called out to them. A warm and jovial voice that immediately pleased Ruby. Peter didn't have time to respond. Emily had already joined them.

— 'You must be Ruby ? I am so happy to meet you. You know, I've heard a lot about you.'

Ruby appreciated the remark. She existed too, Peter had talked about her.

— When I was treating him, when he was delirious from fever, it was you he called for, I remember very well. Did you know that ?'

No, she didn't know. And it felt good to hear it. Emily had that talent. She knew how to find the words that made you feel important. Barely had she arrived that Ruby's resentment and anxiety had disappeared. This reunion, this meeting was a real gift, a precious gift. She immediately knew that Emily would become her friend. The two women talked a lot, while Peter savoured this unexpected happiness. Ruby and Emily were there, near him, laughing together as if they had known each other forever.

Indeed, they quickly became very close, sharing a zest for life and a fierce energy that allowed them to move mountains. Their zest for life, that spark of madness that characterised them, made them irresistible. Peter did not resist. At 74, he had the vague feeling that after a long fifty-year parenthesis, everything was finally going to begin. He felt the desire, the thirst for life, and the urgency too.

PART 4

The harmonica, the trombone,
and the umbrella

Chapter 18

The Angliches

Having become inseparable, Ruby, Emily, and Peter decided to form a trio : 'The Angliches[3].' Peter on trombone, Emily on guitar and piano, Ruby on vocals. They would play Glenn Miller, but not only that. Very quickly, the trio invited Julie Anne to join them. She was delighted to accept and naturally offered her a large house for them to move in together. This shared living arrangement thrilled all four of them, four solitudes coming together. 'The Angliches' bet on friendship and life. They would play wherever they were invited, but most importantly, they would have fun.

That day, they had a meeting at the Hôtel de l'Aiguille.

— 'We're late, and it's my fault. Excuse me, I had forgotten André.'

She caught herself in front of her friends' surprised and vaguely uncomfortable expressions. André ?

---

[3]. Affectionate nickname given by the French to the English

— It's my umbrella. It belonged to him. The day I returned to GrandBourg, the mayor handed it to me. He had found it at the police station shortly after… He decided to keep it to give it back to me one day. Since then, it has never left me. It doesn't open anymore, but it accompanies me everywhere. It protects me, I believe. I'm sure of it.

Emily possessed the beauty of those who refused to let themselves be beaten down. A mix of strength and fragility, a lot of presence, but also a distance that made her a bit mysterious. One immediately fell under her charm. Aware of the emotion she had just stirred in her audience, she continued :

— 'I could use a drink !'

— In fact, tonight, it's champagne ! It's on the house ! Léo and I have a surprise for you. We decided to give our hotel a little facelift. Your story, all three of your stories, touched us.'

— 'Colette ! Since when do you address Mr. Gordon so informally ?' Léo teased, laughing.

— 'Leave it, Léo ! I've been waiting for this moment to be addressed informally for so long !' Peter replied. 'It was time ! I love your language for its ability to show appreciation. I would have liked to address Miller informally.'

— Alright, informal it is ! Actually, I think I just never dared. Regarding the surprise… We decided to rename the hotel. Hôtel de l'Aiguille was not very original. As for the rest, we'll reveal it next month. We won't say more, right Léo ? Oh, and we count on 'The Angliches' to celebrate this rebirth !

In the meantime, I believe Léo has a favour to ask you.'

The young boy blushed and lowered his head. Colette continued :

— He spoke about your story, your stories, to his French teacher. She would like to invite you to her class. He didn't dare ask because we know Emily doesn't like to talk about that period of her life, which we understand.'

Emily looked at the young boy, who reminded her of Fanfan la Mouche. He was a bit like the child she hadn't had but would have loved to have.

— If it pleases you, Léo, I agree. But I would like François to be with us. Because if he hadn't been there… I'll do it for you, but it will be the last time. If Peter, Ruby, and François agree, then I agree.

Peter, of course, accepted. Ruby, however, declined the offer, not feeling legitimate. They insisted. She had also lived through the war, even if it was 'over the Channel'. It was no use. In truth, she didn't want to hear Emily's story, especially about her meeting with Peter. It was a somewhat confused feeling, perhaps the fear of rekindling a deep jealousy that had gnawed at her all these years and which she had finally managed to overcome. She liked Emily a lot, of course, but the septuagenarian Emily, the former Zazou. However, meeting the beautiful Emily with auburn hair, the one in the drawings, no, that was beyond her strength. Her companions did not insist.

— You don't mind, Léo ?'

Peter thought it wise to change the subject.

— 'You want to rename the hotel ? What a funny idea ! What's it going to be called ?

But brother and sister remained silent. It was a surprise.

*

The meeting took place one afternoon. Léo, very proud, was tasked with waiting for his friends at the school gate, while Colette had obtained permission from the teacher and her brother to attend the meeting. Peter, Emily, and François were welcomed as heroes by the impressed teenagers. The three friends were very moved. It was the first time they were going to tell their story. Emily, in particular, seemed very affected. She clung to her umbrella like a lifeline. For a moment, she thought she might have overestimated her strength.

The teacher had prepared everything : the table, the microphone, the visit from the press, the flowers ; the students had brought cakes, and of course, they had prepared thank-you notes. Emily was touched to see that the students had worn their best outfits. With great emotion, the students listened to the three friends' stories. Emily's testimony particularly moved them, especially since she mentioned it was the first time she spoke about it in public. And probably the last. She recounted the arrest, but also the deportation, the long road to hell. She spoke in a white, monotone voice. The rhythm of her sentences echoed the monotonous clacking of the train wheels on the tracks. Finally, she described her arrival, the sinister gate, the ignominy, the selection, the separations, the screams and cries, the fear, the waiting, naked, in the cold rain, the ox nerves, the dogs' fangs, the violence, the smell of blood and death.

The students drank in her words. Peter approached her, took her hand, and placed a long kiss on it. But Emily was far away… Lost in memories she had buried deep within herself. Her two friends became worried.

— Emily…

François had also approached. She turned to him and gave a slight start. She grabbed her umbrella, hugged it to her, and to the surprise of her young audience, brought it to her lips. Then, she pulled herself together and offered a smile she had retrieved from deep within :

— Sorry, I think I've monopolised the conversation…

A student stood up and hugged her. Without a word, she kissed her. It was a slightly rebellious, somewhat gothic girl. Jet-black hair exaggerated makeup ; her teachers said she wasn't very 'academic'. That day, the girl had let down her armour, moved by this woman she admired, who was opening up in front of them.

The three friends then told their story of the meeting, the escape by boat, the fisherman's arrest, the ring found. Emily talked about the Zazous, André, her umbrella, his arrest, his execution, as an example. The students didn't know about the Zazous and were immediately charmed by the idea of resistance through music and 'style.' 'Do not endure,' the motto was sure to appeal to a class of teenagers dreaming of emancipation.

Finally, they talked about their incredible reunion after fifty years and the birth of 'The Angliches.' Marie, the gothic girl, was mesmerised by the old woman. At 15, she already knew this meeting would be pivotal. Emily was proof that one must fight, believe in life, and never give up, 'do not endure.' In an hour, Emily had transmitted her energy and love of life, her refusal of hate. The meeting ended with applause. Marie insisted on giving the bouquet of flowers to Emily. The teacher, who had sensed the young girl's turmoil, agreed.

— Thank you, ma'am, for sharing all this with us. I hope that, shared, these memories will be less heavy to bear. I will never forget this meeting. Is it possible to come to listen to the Angliches ? It would make me so happy.

Emily saw a little of herself in the young student. The same heightened sensitivity, the same latent rebellion, the clothes were different, of course, but the spirit was there. This girl could have been her or the one she never had. She promised to send her an invitation…

The return to Étretat was silent. François and Peter searched for words, afraid of upsetting their friend. Peter was overwhelmed with images, all more horrible than the others. How had she been able to endure the violence and the blows, the hate and the contempt ? One sentence particularly shocked him, and he was afraid to understand. To the 'girl with the piercing' who had asked if she had children, Emily had replied :

— They made sure that was no longer possible.

At the time, he thought she was referring to André's arrest, but then doubt overwhelmed him, became a certainty. Emily had been tortured. He remembered seeing a report on the 'medical' experiments conducted in the camps reserved for women. With all the gentleness he was capable of, he wrapped his arm around his friend and kissed her now white temple.

— I'm sorry, he murmured, and it was like a prayer.

She offered him a weak smile, then straightened up :

— Come on, let's go have a drink !

Chapter 19

Étretat, Hôtel de l'Aiguille, 1995

For several days, the hotel's facade, large and charming, had been playing hide-and-seek with the street. Finally, the big day had arrived. On this occasion, permission had been obtained from the town hall to block the road for an hour. Colette had confided in the mayor, and touched by the story, he decided to participate in the surprise. He was part of the celebration, even deciding to wear his sash for the occasion. Of course, the press and even the television were invited. In fact, the heart of Étretat had decided to be there, out of friendship for Colette and Léo.

— Dear Peter. I believe I can say you are our oldest and most loyal customer. You are part of our childhood memories, back when Suzanne, our grandmother, ran the hotel. And yet… Yet, these past few days, we've felt like we've met you for the first time, discovering who you truly are. Who would have thought that the 'old man,' as I used to call you, had participated in the D-Day landings, had known and played with the great Glenn Miller ? To be honest, I knew nothing of Miller's history, except for his music, which Suzanne adored. Léo and I were very impressed by what you taught us about his end. Finally, we understood why you came to play on the cliff every December 15th, and we decided to join you in this tribute.

Léo, unable to contain himself, interrupted his sister :

— We are happy to welcome you to Hôtel, 'In the Mood'.

The canvas covering the facade finally fell. The immense silhouette of the famous trombonist, stood out on the freshly painted wall. Peter, quite moved, hugged his young friend. It was a magnificent gift his friends had given him. Words failed him. So, he picked up his trombone. Soon the first notes of swing filled the street. Julie Anne, who was in on the surprise, joined him with her double bass. An American tourist passing by, happy to hear music he thought forgotten, invited Ruby to dance. She didn't need much persuading, and soon the music transported her back to a small pub in London, to the days of the Red Lion. The mayor didn't take long to bow before Emily. Léo, meanwhile, led his sister into the street, now turned the dance floor. Just as on the cliff, the onlookers soon joined in and started dancing. The tunes kept coming, no one wanted to part. The weather was beautiful, the spring was mild, and everyone felt content. Life was there, why go elsewhere ? Everyone was aware of living a special moment, one of those moments that allowed happiness to be enjoyed in the present. Yes, happiness was there, in Emily's and Ruby's smiles, who were so different yet united by friendship ; it was there in Julie Anne's forgotten glasses, in Peter's starry eyes. Finally, it was in the somewhat crazy, somewhat unreasonable decision of four friends to create 'The Angliches.'

Thanks to a friend of Julie Anne's, they were able to produce a record. The young Marie, who had a real gift for drawing, was entrusted with designing the cover. This little record was the culmination of the incredible adventure they were living. They gathered to find a name for what they jokingly called 'their album.' Colette suggested, 'Carpe Diem.' The idea was liked and approved. Enjoying the present moment, freeing oneself from the yoke of the past, no longer fearing the future had become their credo. It didn't matter how long it would last ! They had made time and their age their allies because together, they now felt invincible. Never had Julie Anne's house been so joyful, filled with laughter, tenderness, and warmth. Their shared living arrangement reminded the young woman of her student years. Emily smoked weed and didn't hide it, Ruby had a real penchant for beer, English, of course, and Peter began every evening with a glass of Glenmorangie, which he dedicated to his friend. They sometimes quarrelled, but always reconciled. The young musician loved hearing Ruby call their friend 'old codger.' Emily decided that Peter's wardrobe needed a makeover.

How could one dress so poorly !

— He dresses like an old man ! Come on, girls, we have to do something !

Poor Peter, a hardened bachelor, found himself defenceless in the midst of his three friends. But how good it was not to be alone anymore ! He was rejuvenating, even leaving his cane at home.

— Canes are for old people ! He would say, laughing. The transformation was impressive. He had regained that zest for life he had missed so much, finally allowing himself to be happy.

*

December 15, 1995 – What a Wonderful World

Tonight, the Hôtel in the Mood stole the show from the imposing Aval cliff. Even the casino seemed deserted. The trombonist's silhouette was highlighted by a play of lights. In red letters, one could read, 'The Angliches.' For the occasion, the restaurant's dining room had been rearranged. A small stage, numerous chairs, and of course, a space for dancing. Everything was ready. As the sun began to set behind the great cliff, the people of Étretat arrived. The atmosphere was warm and jovial. There was much laughter, some arrived hand in hand. Étretat was happy. Christmas was near, the streets were illuminated. Everyone felt good, protected by the stone giants.

Inside the hotel, it was bustling. People were starting to take their seats. Léo, as the master of ceremonies, ensured everything was perfect. He was helped by Marie, the student Emily had invited. Lately, she was often seen in Étretat, and Léo was never far away. Everything was ready. For the occasion, their longtime friend, François, was invited. Ruby's painter friend was also there. While waiting for the artists to appear, they chatted cheerfully. So many events had happened in recent months ! Colette thought life was beautiful. Discreetly, she took her brother's hand. They were happy together, the two of them. Suddenly, the audience rose to welcome the musicians. The hastily installed curtain opened to reveal the orchestra. They were all there, all four of them.

— Is that really, Peter ?

Léo couldn't believe it. Gone were the tweed jacket and corduroy pants ! Peter had swapped them for a beautiful shirt, a polka dot tie, an anisegreen jacket with a pocket square, and green pants with large pale yellow checks. He was almost unrecognisable. He was accompanied by his three friends. Ruby, true to herself, always extravagant, with bright red hair, a flared skirt, and an orange blouse – she had a bit of a Yvette Horner look, thought Colette. Next came Emily and Julie Anne. Emily remained what she had always been : a Zazou. The pleated skirt was quite short, the little jacket fitted. Of course, the socks were mismatched, her hair was tied back with a ribbon, and her eternal umbrella was there.

Finally, Julie Anne. She too seemed to have gained lightness. Her outfit was colourful, her hair was down, and most importantly, she offered her gaze to the audience. Gone were the dark glasses ; Julie Anne no longer hid. The audience recognised the musician, and some children called out to her.

The evening was dedicated to jazz and, of course, swing. Some chairs were moved to enlarge the dance floor, and everyone started dancing. The younger ones tried to imitate the dance steps of their elders. In the centre of the dance floor were Riton and *Mademoiselle* Paulette. In front of the astonished people of Étretat, the man with braces invited the old maid for a wild rock dance. The little ones clapped their hands, keeping time.

After a short intermission, Ruby, encouraged by her friends, improvised an a cappella rendition of Mercedez Benz. Colette, a big fan of Janis Joplin, was stunned. She didn't know Ruby had such a talent. Later, she would learn that her friend had been at Woodstock in 1969 and had even had the chance to drink a beer with her idol.

— But what do you think, young ones ! The old people of today weren't always old ! And you would be very surprised if we told you everything !' she said, laughing. Besides, it's well known that the current generation is much more uptight than ours ! Look at how reasonable you are !

Listening to her, Marie, the rebel, thought she would have liked to live in that period, to know Woodstock. In school, they had talked about

Jimi Hendrix and his rendition of the American anthem to protest the Vietnam War. Since then, he was part of her pantheon, along with Mandela and Bob Marley. Knowing that Ruby had seen him on stage fascinated her. She promised herself to ask her about it when they were alone.

— Hey, lovebirds ! Come sing with us ! The lovebirds… Blushing and very intimidated, the two teenagers stood up and joined them hand in hand, under Colette's tender smile.

— We're going to sing Imagine together. You agree ? I know you learned it in school.

They sang all five, holding hands. Julie Anne accompanied them on the violin. Colette's eyes filled with tears. She thought she had never been so completely happy. Her friends reached out for her to come to sing the last refrain with them. At that precise moment, she understood they had become her family.

Finally, the concert ended with What a Wonderful World. The four friends had decided to make Louis Armstrong's song their anthem. The world and life could be wonderful. They were living proof.

At the end of the performance, Peter called Léo to the stage :

— Léo, I have a gift for you. I know you've learned to play the harmonica. Here, this is for you.

He handed him a small leather case that the boy recognised immediately.

— I'm giving it to you. You know, it belonged to Glenn. Look, he even signed it. It was his last gift before boarding the plane. I know you'll take care of it. It's yours, but never forget that music is meant to be shared.

There was something solemn and infinitely moving about this gift. Like a relay, the gesture of a grandfather to his grandson. Gravely, Léo took the case, pulled out the instrument, and turning to the picture of Glenn

Miller that his sister had hung on the wall, he began the first notes of In the Mood. Peter needn't worry, he would continue playing for him every December 15th.

Chapter 20

December 15, 1999, off the cliffs

It's a cold and white winter day. Gentle waves lap against the hull of the fishing boat. The cliffs, even more imposing from the sea, stand as privileged witnesses to the scene. In the distance, one can even see Julie Anne's house.

They huddle together, seeking warmth for both body and soul. They all gathered this morning at the port of Fécamp, ready to embark. Julie Anne brought her violin with her, and Léo clutched his harmonica tightly. Ruby, head held high, seemed to be scanning the horizon ; Emily, more than ever, clung to her umbrella. François was also there, close to her, attentive and caring. While the emotion was palpable, it was not sad. Colette took in the scene before her, as if to better absorb it. She looked at her brother and friends with tenderness. Julie Anne, as always when she was moved, chose to hide her gaze behind large sunglasses.

The boat stopped. The gentle swell, the lapping of the waves, brought softness to the moment.

From her shoulder bag, Colette took out the urn and placed it at their feet. Ruby, meanwhile, pulled a bottle of whiskey from her bag, along with five glasses.

— It's Glenmorangie, she said, pouring herself a glass. 'You would have liked it. Your first whiskey, with Miller. Our paths part here, it seems,' she added, downing it in one gulp. 'But I'm used to it. For both of us, it was "The whirlwind of life." We spent our lives losing each other to find each other again,' she continued with a slightly forced laugh, humming the song by Jeanne Moreau. 'You loved that song. Well, goodbye old brother, and who knows, maybe we'll meet again once more…'

She sat down again, not without pouring herself another shot. The others politely declined ; it was still early. Emily's turn came next. She leaned heavily on her umbrella. For the first time, Colette thought she looked her age. She tried to speak, but the words stuck in her throat. She thought of the young man in the cabin, their evening in the school, the stolen kiss before he took the boat to England. She thought of their reunions, the drawing in the beam, the sketchbook, the smile never forgotten. Losing Peter meant saying goodbye to her past.

She also thought of André, André whom she missed terribly at that precise moment. Then, after a deep breath, she started singing their hymn, What a Wonderful World. Her voice trembled a bit, her eyes turned grey, and a tear began to roll down her parchment-like skin. But her smile returned. She clung to François's arm, who helped her sit back down and held her close. He remembered the day she returned to the village, impassive under her mother's jeers and insults.

— Thank you, François, for introducing me to Peter. And most of all, thank you for helping us reunite, she said, resting her head on his shoulder.

Colette stood up in turn. Her first thoughts flew to her grandmother, Peter's great friend, and all those years, all those December 15ths spent together. She hugged Léo tightly, understanding the boy's grief.

— To you, Léo, she murmured softly. 'It's time to say goodbye. The swell is rising, and it's cold.'

Julie Anne took her violin out of its case, and Léo brought his harmonica to his lips. Soon the first notes of Moonlight Serenade mingled with the cries of seagulls as Colette took hold of the urn. The ashes scattered into the mist. Peter had joined Glenn.

A little later, they all gathered at the hotel where Colette had invited them to share a meal. Naturally, they talked about Peter, each sharing their anecdotes. They mentioned the illness, but also the relief of seeing him now 'freed.' Léo hung a photo of the 'Angliches' on the restaurant wall. In it, Peter was beaming, surrounded by the two women who had been the loves of his life.

They talked about life, about the future. Emily and Ruby would continue to live with Julie Anne.

And even if the 'Angliches' disappeared with Peter, they still hoped to be able to sing a little longer.

*

A few years later.

Life resumed its course in Étretat. The seasons and storms, relentless, succeeded one another. When it wasn't the waves, it was the froth of tourists that invaded the small town.

Riri and *Mademoiselle* Paulette were still there, and the covered market continued to delight visitors. At the hotel In the Mood, nothing had really changed. Colette and Léo still welcomed you with the same smile. Léo had become a young man. He chose to stay in Étretat to continue managing the hotel with his sister. Julie Anne still gave music lessons. She now shared her life with Marin, whom she had met a few years earlier in Caen. To the great surprise of her friends, Ruby returned to England a few months after Peter's death. She left one morning, after apologizing to her friends. Continuing the adventure without Peter no longer made sense. She now lived in a retirement home in Walsall, not far from the orphanage where she had grown up with her lifelong companion, where it had all really begun.

It was in 'Peter's room' that Colette found Emily unconscious one afternoon. Tired, she had gone up to rest for a while. She was there, lying on the bed, her umbrella placed next to her. Death had come during her sleep, with gentleness, with…

delicacy. Emily had left very precise instructions for Julie Anne : she was therefore buried in the small cemetery of Étretat, her faithful umbrella in her arms. No ceremony, no cross. To accompany her, François, Julie Anne, Léo, and Colette. On the stone, a simple inscription :

Zah-Zuh-Zaz 4.

It is said today that sometimes, from the top of the Aval cliff when the wind is from the west, at that precise moment when the waves meet the feet of chalk and flint, you can hear a few notes of music. Nostalgic or lively, they accompany the ebb and flow, offerings from the sea to the solid ground. Undoubtedly, the seagulls and gulls hear them, they who never stop dancing.

If you walk on the cliff on December 15th, then perhaps you will have the chance to meet Colette, Léo, and his harmonica.

Author's notes

"Music Above All"

Regarding the night of December 15, 1944…

As is often the case when a wreck is not found, several versions exist concerning the disappearance of Glenn Miller. Off the coast of Fécamp, Étretat : for some, a victim of the weather or an enemy bomber's jettisoning ; for others, he crashed on a beach in Pas de Calais…

Others will say he died in Paris, in 'gallant company'; finally, a fourth version :

Glenn Miller supposedly disappeared in Merville, Normandy…

I leave this mystery to historians to resolve.

After all, what does it matter ! Isn't the music the most important thing ?

Of course, this novel is also dedicated to him.

Notes

The British Cemetery of Douvres-la-Délivrande :
The graves in the La Délivrande military cemetery primarily date from June 6 and the landing on Sword Beach, particularly in the Hautbois and Pierre sectors. Others were later brought from the battlefields between the coast and Caen.

Today, 944 Commonwealth military personnel from the Second World War are buried or commemorated in this cemetery. Sixty-five of the graves are unidentified, but there are special memorials dedicated to a number of victims buried among them. The cemetery also contains 180 German graves.

The presence of this cemetery in this location is explained by the severity of the fighting and the defence of the radar station located not far from there by entrenched German soldiers.

Douvres la Délivrande and Normandy-Tourism

The 9th Battalion :
The 9th (Eastern and Home Counties) Parachute Battalion is an airborne infantry battalion of the

Parachute Regiment, created by the British Army during the Second World War.

The 9th Parachute Battalion participated in two major parachute operations during the second world conflict : the Normandy landing and the crossing of the Rhine in Germany. In Normandy, it was particularly responsible for the attack and disabling of the Merville gun battery, a significant threat to the landing of British troops on Sword Beach.

Source : Wikipedia

Bibliography

Paul Verlaine - *Art poétique*.

Serge Dutfoy - *Glenn Miller BD jazz*, Éditions Nocturne.

Gérard de Cortanze - *Les Zazous*.

By the author : *Une lumière dans la nuit, se souvenir de Clara*, Éditions La Rémanence.

The song *What a Wonderful World*. Lyrics : George David Weiss. Music: Bob Thiele. Performed by Louis Armstrong.

Filmography

Romance inachevée, 'The Glenn Miller Story', a film by Anthony Mann.

Poppies for Clara

For Clara Chompton, and all the deported from Barneville-la-Bertran,

For all of the parachutists of the 9th Battalion of British parachutists

For Erwan, Mélina and Léo

'I learned that courage was not the absence of fear, but the triumph over it.
Nelson Mandela

Preface

At a time when many amateur genealogists began to search for their ancestors, our colleague Christelle Anjou's initiative, to search for reminders of her great-grandmother, could seem commonplace. It was not. In fact, Clara Matthews-Chompton was not an ordinary woman.

In June 1944, like other inhabitants of Barneville-la-Bertran, near Honfleur, she did not hesitate to help British parachutists that had landed in the wood of Saint-Gatien, more than fifty kilometres from their destination: the famous Merville battery. Her gesture is even more courageous when you know that she, herself, is of English origin. As she had the French nationality, she escaped being interned in one of the camps for foreigners from countries at war with the Reich. However, the German occupants remained suspicious of her and thus the risk that she took was that much bigger.

Following a careless action, she is apprehended with six other inhabitants of Barneville-la-Bertran. Thus, Clara Chompton began the ordeal that many women found out about when they were arrested for acting resistant: she went to Fort Romainville, near Paris, then she was deported to the Neue Bremm transition camp, at Sarrebrück and finally she was sent to the Ravensbrück concentration camp from which she never returned.

By honouring her great-grandmother, Christelle Anjou is also paying tribute to all of the people from Lower Normandy – and there were many of them – who did not hesitate, at the risk of losing their freedom and their lives, to bring help, during the night between June 5th and 6th 1944 and in the following days, to the British or American parachutists who had got lost due to errors when they were dropped out of their planes.

Jean Quellien
Professor emeritus of modern history
University of Caen Lower Normandy

Preamble

Above all, I would like to specify that this is not a history book ; I do not have the rigour of a historian.

I just wanted to tell my children the story of a woman, Clara Chompton, and her unfortunate companions. This woman could have stayed in the shadows ; maybe that is actually what she would have preferred. She was one of all of the anonymous people who, seventy years ago, worked so that Peace could return, without looking for glory for themselves. Without asking themselves questions, just because it had to be done. So, today, while we are preparing to commemorate the eightieth anniversary of the allied landing in Normandy, I am pleased to dedicate this small work to her. I wanted people to remember Clara and her gesture. I wanted my children to know who their great-great-grandmother was.

But, like all stories, let us start by setting up the background.

The action took place in Barneville-la-Bertran, a small wooded town in the pay-d'auge, at 5.5 km from Honfleur, not far from Saint Gatien des bois.

Everything began one night. We are in 1944.

It was the night between the 5th and the 6th of June, 1944…

PART 1

1

*'The long sobs of the violins of the autumn
Hurt my heart with a monotonous slowness.'*

During the night from the 5th to the 6th of June, 1944

Amongst the messages broadcast by the BBC on the evening of the 5th of June, 1944, these two lines (translated above) from Verlaine warn the resistance of the imminence of the landing in Normandy. The landing that people had been hoping for and that had already had to be put off for one day because of horrible weather (a storm had surged across the south of England on the evening of the 4th will finally be brought about even though the weather was still gloomy. Come what may.

It was around 11 p.m. when about thirty Dakotas took off from the Broadwell military aerodrome in England. Their objective : Normandy, and more precisely the battery of artillery of Merville-Franceville, north of Caen ; a key spot strategically.

Their aim was to secure the eastern flank of the landing, to protect the troops that would land in the Sword sector (facing Ouistreham-Riva Bella, on the west bank of the Orne River). So that Operation Overload could succeed, that zone absolutely needed to be protected and thus reduce the German cannons of the battery to silence so that, at six o'clock sharp, the Normandy landing could begin. Thus about 650 men took off that night. Unfortunately, the parachuting took place in very bad conditions. Many parachutists drowned in the swamps, weapons were lost and only 150 out of the 600 men planned actually made it to the battery. The rest were spread out over a large zone. The battle was deadly: out of the 150 who arrived, only 80 were still standing at the end of the onslaught.

But the battery had been taken.

2

At around on o'clock in the morning, men belonging to the mortar platoon of the 9th battalion of the British parachutists under the command of the sergeant Edward Smith, seconded by the corporal George Wilson, were parachuted with containers filled with weapons above a fairly vast zone over Barneville la Bertan, at about 35 km from Merville-Franceville.

Many reasons could explain this unfortunate parachuting. One of the aviators of the 32 Dakotas of the 512th squadron that transported the 9th battalion mentioned the following points in his report of the operation 'Overload' that seem important to take into account :

- The signalling lights were off.

- Clouds covered the moon. The flight formation was thus particularly difficult.

- There was a large concentration of about 250 aeroplanes within the *drop zone*. Many crews mentioned almost colliding with other aircraft.

- The Dakota leader (piloted by Commander Coventry) had to try three times to drop off his 'stick', that is to say the line of parachutists that jump out of the same door.

In other reports, it is said that the aeroplanes swerved and suddenly changed course at the moment when they were dropping their load, which caused the parachutists, who were heavily loaded down with gear, to fall into the cabin, which interrupted the drop-off; thus the aeroplane had to fly around again to find the *drop zone* on its own. This, as you can imagine, could not have been easy. Unless the Dakota had aborted the formation in flight (which happened to many planes that night) and got lost even before they reached the French coastline. Lastly, perhaps the pilot confused the Orne with the Touques, a coast side river that flows across the pays d'auge and ends its course in the Channel between Trouville and Deauville ?

The Sergeant Smith in his report tells of this eventful operation.

*

Sergeant Smith's Report

'We took off for Normandy at a quarter past eleven at night on June 5, 1944. At one o'clock, on June 6th, I landed in a wood west of Barneville. I sprained my ankle when I touched the ground. Of course, I immediately tried to make contact with my platoon and to recover our containers. Without success. Thus I remained hidden in this wood until morning, and then I went towards the North. I met a Frenchman who could tell me where I was. I remained in the wood for another 18 hours before going on, this time towards the south. After 2 hours, I found Corporal Wilson, who was hidden in a hedge. We remained hidden until June 7th. At seven o'clock in the evening, we were able to continue on towards the southwest. In the evening, a German sentry shot at us and we had to hide in a field of wheat until dawn. Then we went on to arrive, at around eight o'clock on June 8th in the forest of Saint Gatien des Bois, where we remained until June 9th. It was while going towards Saint Benoît that we met two women who accepted to help us. They came back with their brother and food. We remained hidden in a wood, close to Saint Benoît until June 12th. During these 3 days, the Frenchman brought us food.

On June 12th, at last, a member of the Resistance came to our hideout and took us in a lorry to a barn that was about 3 km from Honfleur where we stayed until June 25th until a group of about 30 members of the Resistance brought us towards a house near Manneville. On July 9th, we were taken in a lorry once again to a barn 4 km north of Beuzeville.'

*

In the end, the two men will manage to regain the United Kingdom at the end of August 1944, after, as we've seen, having been helped by the Resistance and being moved regularly, to cover their tracks. Meanwhile, four or five other parachutists stayed in Barneville la Bertran and were taken care of by families in the community. Clara Chompton was of English origin ; therefore, she served as an interpreter and also helped, like others with the provisioning. It is thus a part of the community who will help the English, to hide them but also to feed them and to provide them with outfits that were 'more discreet'. We must remember the names Rocher, Marie and lastly Quéruel; this book is dedicated to them as well.

One of the parachutists was taken in by the Rocher family in the *ferme des vallées*. The Marie family took in two men, and lastly the Quéruel family hid, as well as some of the men, the containers of weapons. In the end, all of the British parachutists regrouped at this last family's home. One of the members of the Resistance, Mr P Bodeman, who came to the village on June 8th to help the parachutists, later claimed that there were 5 of them. He took them to Englesqueville en Auge to join another group of parachutists that was hidden in a barn.

Of course, the German had been informed very quickly of the parachuting and they were actively searching for these men and also for their weapons. Actually, before June 14th, they took up position on the hills of Englesqueville and marched directly – a bit too directly some would say – towards the barn. The parachutists would be arrested that day. We still do not know anything about the conditions concerning this arrest nor what became of these men.

3

But unfortunately, the story does not end here. After having captured the parachutists, the Germans do not stop at that. The very next day, they begin to search for all those who had helped the English. At first, they go to the farm of the Auger family, and they did this the day after they had captured the English. They search the house, but finding nothing, no weapons and no men, they leave. They go next to Barneville la Bertrand and arrive during the night from June 17th to June 18th. First they wake the mayor to force him to give names and addresses. The mayor, pretending not to understand them, voluntarily gives them information that was very vague. The soldiers force him to follow them. They make him walk barefoot while threatening him with a firearm. They force him to act as a 'guide' and 'interpreter'. Then they went to see the Marie family and arrest the father and his two sons ; then it's the turn of the Quéruel family. At their home, they find the containers of weapons. These were heavy weapons, including mortars, nine-inch mortar bombs that can do a lot of damage. With these weapons, there were also radio sets. The Germans had got their hands onto a real arsenal.

Mr Bodeman had planned to move these weapons (but his plans had been thwarted by the capture of the English), were not intended for the Resistance but were for the British soldiers. We can imagine that it is because of these weapons that the Germans will react with such severity. We must not forget that it was an offence punishable by death to dissimulate weapons. At Barneville la Bertran, most certainly in retaliation, the Germans would arrest 8 people and one inhabitant from Pennedepie, a neighbouring village ; eight people who had helped the parachutists : Leon Quéruel, his son Jean and his son-in-law Émile Ruffin ; Émile Edmond Marie and his two sons Émile Félix Marie and Maurice Marie and also his son-in-law André Lebey, and lastly, Clara Chompton. These 8 people were interrogated and then deported to the Neuengamme and Ravensbrück concentration camps.

Only one of them, Émile Ruffin, would come back in 1945. That is the terrible price that the community of Barneville la Bertran would have to pay for its contribution to the Freedom movement.

Today their names are engraved on a statue dedicated to the dead in the cemetery of Barneville la Bertran, but also in that of Pennedepie. They are also mentioned in the book 'The Memorial book of the victims of Nazism in Calvados' in 2004.

PART 2

4

Dear Clara,

I heard about you for the very first time when I was just a little girl. My grandmother admired you tremendously and she told me all that she could tell a girl of my age. You already seemed like an extraordinary woman, a real heroine, even if I didn't really understand why. I also heard a lot about François, one of your two sons, a brigadier, who also died for France on August 16, 1943. He is buried in the little cemetery in Barneville la Bertrand, not very far from the monument to the dead where your name is. As for your husband Léon Chompton, who died on February 19, 1944, he did not know the story that I have chosen to tell. You were thus a widow, and you only had your second son, Robert, and his young wife for the family. My grandmother spoke of you with a lot of respect and emotion and I've often regretted not knowing more about you. But, it is often difficult to speak of the war and of the dark years for the Elderly… She gave me pictures of you and even a lock of your hair, like a relic that she had kept for years in a small envelope. I think that it was while listening to her that the idea for this piece of work came to light. She even encouraged me to write your story.

It was in 2011 that Marcel Dupuis contacted me. Owner of the Manoir des Vallées where one of the paratroopers was hidden by the Rocher family, a history buff, he was passionate about the history of these paratroopers and the disastrous fate of the victims of Barneville. He therefore embarked on research, constantly finding the history of the paratroopers and the deportees of Barneville-la-Bertran. He was the one who contacted me I was invited, as your direct descendant to attend the inauguration of a commemorative plaque in tribute to the deported of Barneville la Bertran, at the Battery Museum of Merville-Franceville.

Since then, I have met many people, first in Barneville la Bertrand where you left a living memory. Lately, I even talked to a man who had known you. When he was introduced to me, he could not stop himself from crying as he held my hands. His emotion was such that I trembled as well. He was noticeably pleased to learn about my project.

A little while later, I met one of your nephews, Claude. Our meeting was even more extraordinary that is was by pure luck. It was at the Book Fair in Alençon, in June 2013. I was presenting one of my books, when, while talking to one of the authors sitting at my table, I discovered that she was my distant cousin. Her father, Claude, remember you specifically and he told me emotionally about his childhood holidays in Barneville la Bertran with his cousins François and Robert, in the manager's house. This amazing meeting was like a flash. I had to continue ! Another emotional meeting was the one with Mrs André Rocher, who did not know you, but who had heard about you for all of her life from her husband and mother-in-law, Mrs Denise Rocher. Yes, all of these people helped bring me closer to you and you seem more familiar to me every day. Perhaps, one day, I will go to Walsall, in the United Kingdom, where you were born, to get to know you even better and maybe even meet people from our family.

Until then, I went in search of landscapes that were familiar to you, to see you lovely house, the one where you were happy, with your husband, Léon and your sons, François and Robert; the one where everything stopped, one day in June 1944. The shutters were closed when I went by. But the stream still flows behind the house… and your memory is still extremely present.

But let us go back to our story, to your story.

5

Barneville la Bertrand, June 19, 1944
5 o'clock in the morning

The day rose slowly over Barneville la Bertrand on this June 19th. Everything was off in the pretty half-timbered manager's house. The shutters were closed, the lights were off. The house was silent. Perhaps it was still asleep. If you prick up your ears, you can hear the bubbling sound of the little stream that flows behind the house ; the same one that made the children happy during the holidays when they would fish for crayfish with their trousers rolled up their calves when the cousins would come to play when the weather was fine. It was a long time ago ; it was… before. In fact, if today everything is calm it is only in appearance. We are June 19, 1944, and soon, in a few minutes, German soldiers would come to arrest the tenant of this place, Mrs Clara Chompton. Indeed, there they come, knocking at the door. Clara is alone. Thankfully, Robert, her son, and his young wife Suzanne are absent. The young couple, who has recently got married, has just moved to Vasouy, near Honfleur. In any case, it is her, Clara, whom they came for.

Unceremoniously, they take her to Honfleur, to the Kommandatur. They had questions to ask her, about the British soldiers that she may have helped. And also, Clara Chompton, born Matthews, even though she had obtained French nationality, was of English origin, and naturally, that was not in her favour in this month of June 1944. We are in the middle of the battle of Normandy and the German soldiers are on the war path.

Was Clara the victim of a denunciation ? Of thoughtlessness ? Was it a mistake ? All of the above are possible. But, unfortunately, yet again, there are several versions.

6

'Ask Clara Chompton, she's the one who knows everything.'

A bit of research helped me to find out more about the arrest and tragic end of my great-grandmother, in particular thanks to her son, Robert and the report that he wrote on these events in 1945 (statements given on January 29, 1945, in the National Gendarmerie of Honfleur). That same day, as soon as the arrest of his mother was announced, Robert went to his parents' house. He could only take note that the house had been looted and that all of his mother's jewellery had been stolen. He tried to see her many times at the *Kommandatur* and finally was permitted to by the sentinel. But they could not talk because they were under close scrutiny. Robert went back the very next day on the pretext of bringing her food. Until then, he had been careful not to say what his family ties to Clara were. She managed to tell him that he was also being searched for and also that they were waiting for her to give up the names of the other members of the network. If she did not tell them, she would be shot.

In spite of the danger, Robert would return to the *Kommandatur* one more time, determined to find out who had denounced his mother. In fact, it seemed that one sentence was at the origin of her arrest: '*Ask Clara Chompton, she's the one who knows everything.*' This time, he decided not to hide his identity. Of course, they let him in, somewhat surprised that he would 'jump into the lion's den'. This allowed him to speak with his mother but also to talk to the others who had been arrested with her, for the same case. 'My mother assured me that she had not given anyone else up, that she had "taken it all for herself". That day, Robert Chompton, after kissing his mother one last time – for the last time – took advantage of the sentinel taking Mr Marie outside to do his business to slip away. Two, or three days later, after watching his mother's departure from afar, my grandfather left with his young wife to hide in the Orne, where they would stay until the liberation.

Of course, in between, Robert followed the stages of his mother's journey. Thus, he would learn that she had been taken first to Evreux then to Romainville.

7

Robert Chompton lost track of his mother at the Romainville Fort and thought naturally that she, like many others, after having been tortured in the rue des Fossés, must have been shot.

On July 18, 1944, Clara was deported from Paris to Sarrebruck. That day, sixty-five of them left. From there, she was transferred to Ravensbrück, with the number 47,333, one amongst the 8,000 French who were deported. I have tried to follow her, to reconstruct her last voyage.

The prisoners were usually taken at dawn from the Romainville Fort. In a bus, they were taken to Paris. Sometimes they were allowed to bring along some of their things. The luckiest was given a package from the Red Cross, including a little butter, a bit of sausage, a few biscuits, some chocolate and perhaps a little bread and pâté. Other times, and most often, they had nothing.

What about you, Clara ? Were you given this last bit of "sweetness" before knowing the hell ?

The women were then put on-board the third-class wagons that had wire netting over the windows. These "cell wagons' were linked to the regular trains on the Paris-Berlin train line.

Did you try, like so many of your tormented companions, to throw a message for your son Robert and for Suzanne through the wires ? Many of these messages, picked up by anonymous hands and friends, arrived at their given destination. These messages were from mothers, wives, daughters or fiancées who were trying to give a clue, or to reassure their loved ones, or perhaps just say a last goodbye. The arrival at Neue Bremm marked the beginning of the experience of concentration camps. The women were unloaded, pushed without consideration. Upon their arrival they were received by the soldiers' yells, the dogs' growling and teeth and sometimes they were even spit upon by the civilians and even by children who were raised to hate the deported. All of the testimonies of the surviving women say the same thing. They witnessed, upon their arrival in camp, scenes of unspeakable violence.

For you, Clara, it was only a stop on the way. Your real destination was the Ravensbrück camp, in northern Germany, near Furstenberg. How long did you stay in Neue Bremm ? We don't really know. In general, the deported stayed there for only about twenty days. We know that during the summer of 1944, the New Bremm camp allowed for the formation of bigger and bigger convoys, thus optimising the transport towards Ravensbrück, this was one of the last workings of the repressive deportation.

The reason for their arrest was also taken into consideration. A member of the Resistance, of English origin, Clara was 58 years old, of rather frail constitution : these made up quite a few reasons to expect the worst. In fact, she died on November 1st, 1944. Of course, the circumstances surrounding her death are unknown.

I often think of you, dear Clara, of Lucie and Raymond Aubrac, Jean Moulin… and all of these important people that everyone knows about. i also think about the anonymous people, who were so important and who were so numerous. Sometimes, I find myself wondering if I would have had your nerve. Would I have 'stood' the blows and the torture, the hardships and the insults of the Rue des fosses, without speaking ? I think of Mathilde, the resistant in the novel *The Army of Shadows* (l'Armée des ombres in French) by Joseph Kessel, of her nerve and strength. You were like that.

I would like you to know that I am infinitely proud of you, of all of you, thanks to whom my children, today, can grow up in a country at peace.

PART 3

Morts pour avoir aidé des hommes du 9ème Bataillon de Parachutistes Britanniques

They died for having helped men of the 9th Parachute Battalion

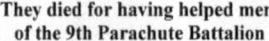

Dans la nuit du 5 au 6 juin 1944, un groupe de parachutistes du 9ème Bataillon est largué par erreur sur la commune de Barneville-la-Bertran près d'Honfleur, à 30 km de l'objectif de la Batterie de Merville.
Ces hommes appartiennent à une section du peloton de mortiers du Bataillon commandée par le Sergent Edward SMITH, secondé par le Caporal George «Tug» WILSON.
Au matin, quatre des parachutistes dispersés sont recueillis et dissimulés par des habitants du village, qui rassemblent aussi les armes lourdes contenues dans des containers.
Quelques jours plus tard la résistance prend en charge les parachutistes et les fait quitter la commune. Les 18 et 19 juin, les soldats allemands arrêtent sept habitants de Barneville-la-Bertran et un habitant du village voisin de Pennedepie, accusés d'avoir apporté leur aide aux parachutistes.
Tous sont déportés en Allemagne, dans les camps de concentration de Neuengamme et de Ravensbrück.

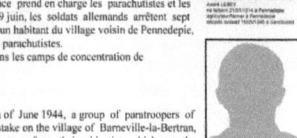

During the night of the 5th and 6th of June 1944, a group of paratroopers of the 9th Battalion was dropped by mistake on the village of Barneville-la-Bertran, near Honfleur, at 20 miles (30 km) away from their objective which was the Merville Battery. These men belonged from to a section of the Battalion's mortar platoon, commanded by Sergeant Edward SMITH, seconded by Corporal George "Tug" WILSON.
In the morning, four of these paras were helped and hidden by inhabitants of the village. The villagers also regrouped the heavy arms witch had dropped in the containers. A few days later, Résistance underground fighters moved the paras out of the village. On the 18th and 19th of June, German troops arrested seven inhabitants of Barneville-la-Bertran and one inhabitant of the nearby village of Pennedepie, accusing them of heaving helped British paratroopers.
All were deported to Germany, in the concentration camps of Neuengamme and Ravensbrück.

Sept mourront/Seven died : Clara CHOMPTON
Emile MARIE père
Emile MARIE fils
Maurice MARIE
André LEBEY
Léon QUERUEL
Jean QUERUEL

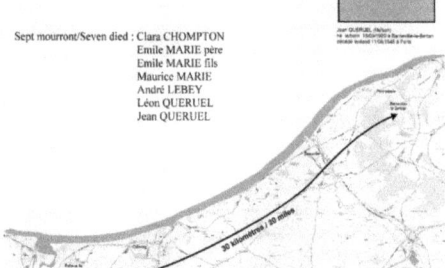

*Commemorative plaque,
Merville battery*

8

The Battery Museum, Merville-Franceville, June 4, 2011We are June 4, 2011.

My husband and I have been invited to the Battery Museum in Merville-Franceville to the inauguration of a commemorative plaque in the honour of the deported from Barneville la Bertran. I have been invited as the direct descendant of one of the victims. What is expected of me ? Will I be expected to speak ? What should I wear ? All these questions and more bounced around in my head. I don't want to admit it, but I'm nervous, as if History had invited me. When I arrive, I am welcomed by Mrs Dagon, the director of the museum and by Mr Dupuis. I am surprised and touched by the reception that I have been given and, I must admit that I cannot help but be touched by the solemnity of the ceremony. Veterans, Sergeant Smith's comrades-in-arms come to say hello to me, a few people that I am presented to as Clara Chompton's great-granddaughter take me in their arms and talk to me about my great-grandmother.

I am asked if I have any children, people want to see their pictures, people are wonder-struck to see that my daughter, aged 16 at the time, looks like her great-great-grandmother. It is true that the resemblance is striking, I had already seen it.

During the ceremony, I am invited to be on the right-hand side of the platform. I am a bit (very) uncomfortable, it is a great honour, but I finally accept. So I join Mr Jean AUBERT, himself (the son-in-law of Emile MARIE who died on April 15, 1945, in Meppen-Versen, the brother-in-law of Emile MARIE-son who was deported and of whom all trace was lost and of Maurice MARIE who died on April 27, 1945, in Sandbostel) and Mr Thomas AUBERT (Emile MARIE's great-grandson). We listen to the speech given by Mr O Paz, the mayor of Merville-Franceville and the President of the Franco-Britannic Battery Association of Merville. After a minute's silence, which seemed never-ending to me, it is up to me to do the honours of placing a bouquet of flowers for Clara, in bunker n°2 of the Museum of Merville-Franceville.

I am moved to meet Mr Tom Hugues, a veteran of the 9th Battalion. We gather our thoughts while looking at the photos of these people that the Museum of Merville-Franceville has chosen to honour. I am moved by this image, surrounded by all of these veterans who stay close to me and who are visibly touched by my presence.

When everyone's tongues have loosened up, they talk to me about the extraordinary woman who Clara Chompton was. Of course, she is not unknown to me. But this time, I am told their story, the story about the eight of them. I think of the Marie family, of which none of the men would return; the sons were so young… Maybe that was the day when I realised exactly what the saying 'Died for France' really meant. It was at this moment that I came up with the idea to write this short text as a tribute and L'harmonica le trombone et le parapluie, my novel.

To conclude the ceremony, we climbed aboard the Dakota that was exposed in the Museum. This American aeroplane is a DC-3. It played an important role in the Second World War. Used as a transporter, to pull gliders; it was also used to release the parachutists. It was one of these that, 67 years earlier, had flown the 9th Battalion over Barneville-la Bertran.

Epilogue

80 years later.
What happens now ?

I hope that these unpretentious few lines will allow you to know your story and that of your unfortunate companions that I would like to name : Mr Emile Marie father, Mr Emile Marie son, Mr Maurice Marie, Mr André Lebey, Mr Léon Quéruel and Mr Jean Quéruel. Thus, you will continue to exist and we will not forget you.

I cannot help but think of Philippe Grimbert and of his novel 'Un Secret' (a secret). In this novel, he offers a grave to a brother deceased after being deported. I like this idea. Words that fix ideas and make them exist. Finally, I especially hope that our younger generations will remain vigilant while trusting in life. It is important not to forget that Freedom and Democracy are something that must always be defended, tooth and nail, and that we must never drop our guard. Ever. You only have to listen to the world around you to hear the hatred growling here and there to be convinced.

It is the younger generation who are the keepers of this fragile equilibrium. It is important to remember and to be grateful to those who risked and sometimes even gave up their lives for this freedom that it is so important to defend. To know, to understand and finally to act.

For my part, my children will learn the story of their great-great-grandmother and her companions.

Because Clara's story is also their history.

References

John Smith's Report

Robert Chompton's Report

Le journal de la bataille de Normandie, J Quellien

Le mémorial des victimes du nazisme en Basse-Normandie, J Quellien

Les femmes déportées via le camp de Sarrebrück — Neue Bremm P-E Dufayel

Site « Mémoire vivante », trimestre n° 61, juin 2009
Comme un petit coquelicot ((Raymond asso, Claude Valéry, Marcel Mouloudji

Thanks for "The little boy and the paratrooper"

My heartfelt thanks go to :
Neil Barber, who honored me with a foreword. Thank you for your kindness and availability.

Thanks to my friend, the Franco-British author Martin Long, for his translation.

Thank you to Serge Dutfoy, comic book artist and jazzman, for his drawing "In the Mood."

Thanks to Amélie Quermont for her professionalism and availability.

And finally, thank you to my editor Nathalie Jaussaud-Obitz at Éditions In Octavo, with whom the adventure of Peter Gordon began.

Thanks for "Poppies for Clara"

As for me, all I have left to do is thank Mrs André Rocher, Mrs Dagorn, Mrs Anne-Sophie Boisgallais, my grandmother Mrs Suzanne Godin, Mr Dupuis, Aubert, Bernard, the mayor of Barneville la Bertran, Claude Boisgallais, Mr O Paz, the Mayor of Merville-Franceville and the President of the Merville Battery Association, Mr M Abraham, of the Battery Association of Merville, Mr G Marshall, the first deputy mayor of Barneville la Bertan, Mr T Lea, the President of the Veterans' Association of the 9th Battalion of the British Parachutists., Kieran Pommier and my son Léo, my interpreters and finally, Mr Jean Quellien, a historian for the valuable information that he provided. Without them, nothing would have been possible.

Since then, some of the people who accompanied me on this wonderful adventure are no longer with us. My thoughts go in particular to Claude, your nephew, to Mr Jean Aubert and Mrs Louise Rocher with whom I have discussed and shared a lot. Of course, I also have a thought for the veterans of the 9 è battalion, met at the time but who are no longer here to tell and testify. Times certainly pass but their memory remains and will remain.

Finally, I want to thank Mrs Agathe Letellier for this wonderful initiative: to dedicate a day of remembrance in tribute to Clara, at the manor of Apreval, in Pennedepie. This Memorial Day moves me and I will be proud to be there with Mélina, her great-great-granddaughter.

> *'Like a little poppy, my soul*
> *A tiny poppy.'*
> May 2024

By the same author

De Vous à Moi, La Rémanence, (testimony)

Mémoire de Babouchka, La Rémanence (life story, ghostwriting)

Les Fleurs du lac, La Rémanence (novel)

Le cabanon jaune, La Rémanence (novel)

Une lumière dans la nuit, La Rémanence (life story)

La fugue de Julie Anne, In Octavo Editions (novel)

L'harmonica le trombone et le parapuie, In Octavo

D'encre et de pierre, La Rémanence (collection of short stories and poems)